LOVE *and* MISUNDERSTANDING

a novel by

T. J. Siemens

FriesenPress

Suite 300 - 990 Fort St
Victoria, BC, Canada, V8V 3K2
www.friesenpress.com

ISBN
978-1-4602-8032-4 (Hardcover)
978-1-4602-8033-1 (Paperback)
978-1-4602-8034-8 (eBook)

1. Fiction, Romance, Historical

Distributed to the trade by The Ingram Book Company

*"There are as many forms of love
as there are moments in time."*

JANE AUSTEN

PROLOGUE

1842

It *was an unusually bright*
day in the town of Portsmouth, as many of the civilians awaited an
immigrant family from Germany's emergence from their ship, which
had just recently docked. Among the crowd was my family, and our
friends the Caldwell family. A hush fell over the boisterous crowd as
a middle-aged man emerged, followed by a woman and two children. My father, being the ever-so-polite gentleman he is, extended
his hand to the man.

"Welcome to Portsmouth. I am the Governor, Sir
Charles Gilmore."

"Jonathan, do stand up straight," my mother whispered, as she
poked me in the ribs.

"This is my wife, Elizabeth," my father continued, "our sons,
Vincent and Jonathan, and our daughter, Caroline."

"Heinrich Hoffman," Mr. Hoffman said, shaking Father's hand.
"This is my wife, Johanna, our son, Alexander, and our daughter, Helene."

He spoke with a rich German accent that made it difficult to
understand certain words. He had short slicked-back hair and a

ridiculous-looking moustache that resembled a grey caterpillar. His face was nearly emotionless as he spoke with my father, and it seemed as if he were unable to smile.

Mrs. Hoffman was a short and stout woman who appeared genuinely happy to be here. Her light brown hair was pulled back into a neat bun, and placed atop was a black bonnet. Her eyes were a beautiful bright shade of blue, which I had to say was her best feature.

The boy named Alexander appeared to be nearly eleven, while his sister, Helene, appeared to be six years of age, a year younger than myself. As the young Helene's eyes ventured about, taking in the unfamiliar scenery, I began to take notice of how extraordinary she was. Although she did have some strikingly beautiful features, I could not help but notice how frail she looked. Her skin had nearly no colour in it whatsoever, and if I had not known better, I would have said that she was made of porcelain.

"It is a pleasure to make your acquaintance, Mr. Hoffman," Father replied, as he motioned for Mr. Caldwell to come forward. "This is my close friend Joseph Caldwell."

"It is a pleasure," Mr. Caldwell said, shaking Mr. Hoffman's hand. "This is my wife, Margaret, and our children, Matthew, James, and Mary."

Mr. Hoffman looked him up and down. "Are you a *Hochwürden?*" he asked, fumbling for the correct word.

"I beg your pardon?" Mr. Caldwell questioned, clearly unsure of what Mr. Hoffman had just called him.

"You must forgive my father. He is still adjusting to the English language," Alexander explained. "I believe he asked if you were a reverend."

"Oh," Mr. Caldwell nodded his head in understanding. "I am indeed the reverend of the local church."

As they all began to talk, I glanced over at my friend Matthew Caldwell, whom I noticed was wearing a mischievous grin on his face. I watched as he reached into his coat pocket and took out a small, wooden slingshot. He then bent down and picked up a few large rocks. At first I had wondered what he would do with the rocks, but I learned soon enough as he began to pelt Miss Hoffman with them. To this very day, I can still recall her scream.

"Helene, what is the matter?" her mother asked, glancing over at her.

"That boy is throwing rocks at me!" she exclaimed, pointing to my friend.

"Matthew Caldwell! How many times have I told you not to play with that slingshot?" Mrs. Caldwell yelled, seizing the slingshot. "Apologize this instant!"

"Sorry," he grumbled.

The young Miss Hoffman shifted closer to her mother as they continued on with their conversation. Without a doubt, it was done in fear of getting hit again. At that moment I had felt sorry for her. I understood my friend's character better than most others, and I knew that he would make her life miserable for many years to come.

And in those carefree childhood years, I had actually cared about the issue. Life had still looked somewhat bright to me back then. I did not realize that I would lose all interest in the unfortunate little girl who had angered Matthew Caldwell.

CHAPTER ONE

1855

As 1 walked through the cor-
ridor, my eyes came to rest upon a large room lined with creamy silk-draped windows. From where I had stopped to examine the room, I could see that my ever-so-charming brother, Vincent, was already dancing with a young lady from church. Naturally, he had become engaged to a woman of noble birth at infancy; however, he had made it no secret that he did not wish to be married. I suppose you could say that he was considered the town flirt. I could not blame him for his actions, for I myself found the idea of an arranged marriage simply repugnant. However, because of his actions, Mother's high expectations were forced onto me.

While I walked along the sidelines of the room, I began to search for my closest friend. The very boy who had once been known as a natural-born trouble maker. On the rare occasion that I happened to think back on the past, I realized how drastically we had both changed since then. I had become a gloomy pessimist and he had become a love-struck fool.

I spotted my friend, who was hiding behind a large plant and appeared to be looking for someone.

"Matthew, there you are," I greeted him.

"Jonathan," he said, briefly acknowledging me before continuing his search.

"Who are you looking for?" I asked, following his gaze.

"No one," he denied. "I was only counting the number of couples."

I sighed, "The Hoffmans have not arrived yet."

"Why would I be looking for the Hoffmans?" he tested.

"It is rather obvious that you are waiting for Miss Helene Hoffman."

"All right, you caught me," he gave up. "Please tell me it is not as obvious to others."

I shrugged, "Perhaps they think that you are planning to pelt them with rocks."

He rolled his eyes. "Was she even invited to this ball?"

"I was informed that everyone received an invitation. Whether or not they choose to attend is their own decision, however." Just then, the Hoffman family entered the ballroom, followed by the Abbott family.

I glanced briefly at Matthew and noticed that his eyes were already glued to Miss Hoffman. I rolled my eyes in annoyance, for I knew that tonight would be no different than any other. At the many balls that had been hosted over the years, Matthew had been known to spend his entire night staring at her, while I would run around after him, ensuring that he did not accidentally light the house on fire.

"Are you going to ask her to dance with you tonight, or will you chicken out as usual?" I teased.

"Yes, I will do it tonight," he assured himself, as he straightened his cravat, cleared his throat, and patted down his light brown hair. "How does my hair look?"

"Do I look like a hairdresser to you?" I asked in annoyance. "It looks fine."

With that, he stepped out from behind the plant and made his way to the other side of the room. I leaned back against the wall and let out a small sigh. Matthew tended to become nervous around Miss Hoffman. At times I could hardly believe that such an obsession could develop out of hatred, and although I could not see how an opinion could change like that, it did not seem to concern my friend.

"Are you hiding from someone?" my brother asked, coming toward me.

"You are most hilarious, Vincent," I said, with a sense of sarcasm.

"Why are you not dancing?" he asked. "There are dozens of pretty girls here. Surely there must be at least one you find agreeable."

"I see that you have found many agreeable women. You have danced with nearly every woman in the room, and yet you have not even danced with your own fiancée."

Vincent fell silent for a brief moment, and then explained, "I shall have plenty of occasions to dance with her when we are married. Nonetheless, you should dance as well. I am certain that I could find you an excellent dancing partner. I cannot think of a single woman who would not jump at the chance to dance with you. Perhaps I could ask Miss Abbott."

"I prefer to stay here and wait for Matthew. Besides, Miss Abbott appears to be far too busy dancing with James."

"All right, be a wall-flower," he said, as he began to walk away. "However, one day you will find someone with whom you will want to dance the entire evening."

"I highly doubt that," I mumbled to myself.

I stayed behind the plant for a while, watching couples circle round and round, until I grew weary and decided to go check up on Matthew. As I made my way across the ballroom, squeezing past numberless dancing couples, I finally spotted him. He stood in a corner and seemed to be looking for someone again.

"Who are you looking for now?" I asked

"I am still looking for Miss Hoffman. We have been playing hide-and-seek for the past five minutes," he said.

"What do you mean you have been playing hide-and-seek?"

"I have spotted her numerous times, but by the time I get to her she is gone," he explained. "Do you think that she could still be angry with me over how I treated her as a child?"

"I am sure that she has forgotten all about it. She is most likely being dragged about by her father," I assured him.

"Perhaps you are right," he said, beginning his search again. "Help me look for her."

I sighed and followed after him. We searched outdoors, indoors, and down all of the corridors, yet we could not find her anywhere. It was as if she had disappeared into thin air. Then, after we had finally given up and returned to our original hiding spot, we found Miss Hoffman standing on the exact spot we had first seen her, speaking with her brother and his wife, Charlotte.

"You had better go ask her before she vanishes again."

He took a few seconds to gather his courage before finally walking up to her. "Miss Hoffman, may I have this next dance?" he asked.

Her eyes widened with surprise, "I am afraid that I have already promised the next dance to someone else."

I winced in pain as I heard her words. Surely that had bruised his ego a great deal. He stood there frozen in place as she excused herself and rushed off. I quickly pulled him out into the garden, knowing that his temper would set off at any moment.

"I am such a fool! She was most likely standing there the whole time and I never noticed!" he fumed, kicking a large stone. "Ow!" he winced in pain.

"Calm down; there will be other balls. Perhaps she does not feel the same way after all," I said, trying to lighten the mood.

"Why would she not love me? I am handsome and of good wealth!" he exclaimed.

I shook my head, "There is that alter ego again."

Out of all the foibles that my friend possessed, his alter ego and temper were by far the worst. He could be kind and considerate one moment, but then he would turn into a hot-headed buffoon. I could not believe that such a person could be the son of a minister, and it was for that reason that I dreaded to think of how a marriage with him would fare.

"Forgive me for letting my temper get the best of me," he said, beginning to calm down. "I am just disappointed that I missed my chance to dance with her."

"I am certain that you will have more opportunities, into which you will most likely drag me somehow."

He laughed, "You are a good friend, Jonathan."

"At times I think I am too good of a friend, considering how much grief you have caused me," I replied, as I headed back inside.

"Perhaps you are," he whispered, and followed after me.

CHAPTER TWO

I could feel the wind brush against my face as we approached the Gilmore manor. For a moment, there was a gust of warmth in the chilly autumn air before it quickly vanished. Then, as the carriage came to an abrupt halt, my father got out and began to help me and my mother down from the carriage.

I began to look about the estate, admiring the immensity of splendour. A large fountain stood in the middle of the yard and was surrounded by flowers of every type and colour. The gardeners scurried about, trimming hedges and watering flowers as if everything had to be perfect.

"Come along, Helene," my mother called from the doorway.

"Yes, Mama," I replied, following after her.

As I stepped inside, I took in the glorious sight before me. The floors were of checkered marble and the walls of creamy paste. The ceiling was painted with a beautiful nature design and tall columns lined the room. From what I had been told, the house was supposed to have more than twenty bedrooms, two large kitchens, and the largest ballroom in Portsmouth. My observation was then cut short by two servants who entered the room. One of them took our coats, handing them to the other before escorting us upstairs.

"You will find Miss Gilmore in the music room," he said, as he began to escort my mother and father down the opposite corridor.

You see, I had been taking music lessons once a week from the Governor's daughter, Caroline, since the age of twelve, and by now I had become accustomed to this process.

I made my way down the endless corridor of doors and windows, stopping once in a while to look out at the breathtaking scenery. Once I had found myself in front of the correct door, I knocked gently and waited for a few moments before Caroline called for me to enter.

"Helene!" exclaimed my friend, Louise, as she rushed over to me. "We must discuss the ball last night."

I considered Louise to be a close friend of mine, and although our friendship often wavered, she was really the only friend I had. "Louise," I greeted her with a smile, as she took my hand and led me to the sofa.

"I danced with James four times!" she swooned. "He is an excellent dancer in comparison to that clumsy buffoon, Mr. Seymour."

"I danced with him as well and I was fortunate enough not to have my foot stepped on more than once," I giggled.

She giggled as well, "Who else did you dance with?"

I breathed a silent sigh of relief and thanked God that she had not taken notice. Surely, if she had seen me refuse Matthew Caldwell, she would have lectured me about it. "Well," I muttered, trying to recall whether I had danced with anyone else. The problem was that I had spent most of my time attempting to get away from Matthew, whom I was quite certain had been following me the entire evening.

"Helene, you are such a wall-flower! Unless you wish to spend your days alone, and without a penny to your name, you had best start socializing more!" she complained. "The Caldwell family is hosting their annual derby next week. My family happens to know many of the contestants. Perhaps I should introduce you to a few of them."

"All right, Louise," I relented. "However I refuse to meet more than three."

"Only three? I shall have to choose the most charming ones then."

Caroline cleared her throat, "Louise, I believe your mother and father are waiting for you."

"Of course." With that she headed to the door. "I will see you next week, Helene." Then she was gone.

"Now, shall we begin the lesson?" Caroline asked.

I nodded my head and took a seat in front of the piano. I could play quite well, even though Caroline still corrected me on a few mistakes every now and then. There were even times when she would join me and we would play a duet. I had never heard her raise her voice at me, even in the most difficult lessons. All things considered, I found her to be a wonderful teacher.

The public had been known to whisper behind her back about the fact that she was twenty-four years of age and yet remained unmarried. I knew very little of what had happened to make her decide to never marry, but I was very fond of her nonetheless. Perhaps that was because I had little desire to get married myself. I believed that I would much rather play piano all day than spend my time slaving away over a man who did not care for me at all.

"May I ask you a question?" Caroline asked suddenly.

"Of course."

"Why is it that you do not tend to socialize much with others?"

"I do have quite a few reasons; however, at the heart of it all, I am much too insecure about my way of speech."

"Why?" she asked curiously. "What is wrong with your way of speech?"

"Although I have lived here in England for nearly thirteen years, my German accent can still be heard when I say certain words, and besides ... I am not nearly as charming as Louise is," I explained.

"You should not think so lowly of yourself, Helene. You are a beautiful young woman. You have a figure that most women, myself included, would give anything for," she claimed. "You should also stop trying to conceal your German heritage. It is simply who you are, and it should not stop you from socializing with others."

I smiled slightly, "I suppose that you are correct. Perhaps I truly am nothing but a wall-flower."

"You sound so much like my brother, Jonathan," she commented.

"I hardly believe that proud peacock could ever feel outcast," I retorted.

"Proud peacock?" she repeated. "I may not know my brother well, but I certainly do not view him as proud. I believe that he is more misunderstood than proud."

"Really?" I questioned in disbelief.

I had always thought of Jonathan as an arrogant snob who did not consider a single woman to be worthy of the honour of dancing with him. I had never thought that it may be because he felt uncomfortable in a large crowd.

"I believe that if the two of you were to put your differences aside, you would find that you have more in common than you think."

"I doubt that I will ever have an opportunity to find out for myself. I do not believe he has ever spoken more than two words to me," I said, as I ceased playing the piano.

To be completely honest, I was all right with that. I had seen so many other women drool over him that I had come to find the idea of getting to know him completely repugnant. Of course, I could see why they drooled over him. He was indeed very handsome with his short dark-brown hair and smoky grey eyes; however, I did not believe that opinions should be based on appearances alone.

"He is not very comfortable speaking to people he does not know well; although he does tend to confide in his closest friend, Matthew Caldwell, more than others."

"Yes, I have noticed that," I admitted. "Tell me, how long have they been friends?"

"I believe that they met as infants, so they have most likely been friends since about the age of three."

"I find it amazing that friendships can begin at such a young age."

"Have you never had a friend like that?" she asked.

"I am afraid that the longest friendship I have had is with Louise," I explained. "There was a boy with whom I was quite close as a child, but it did not last."

"I am deeply saddened to hear that," she claimed. There came a knock on the door just then. "Come in."

"You must forgive my intrusion," the servant apologized, opening the door slightly. "Miss Hoffman, your parents have finished their tea and are waiting for you."

"You may tell them that I will join them directly."

"As you wish," the servant nodded and left us.

As I went to go, Caroline grabbed onto my hand to stop me from going, "You need not feel outcast and alone, Helene. God shall never leave you, nor forsake you, and I believe that one day he will bring into your life someone who will bring you out of your shell."

I managed to smile slightly at her before leaving the music room and making my way down the endless corridor of doors and windows again. "I highly doubt that," I muttered to myself.

CHAPTER THREE

The world flashed before my eyes as I raced my liver chestnut thoroughbred along the long, winding forest trail. It was at moments like these that I could forget about what others thought of me and simply be myself. It felt as if I were on top of the world without a single soul there to bother me. Unfortunately, I then remembered that I happened to be racing against my occasionally annoying friend on his dark bay mustang.

He was an excellent rider to be sure; however, you could clearly tell that he was trying too hard. As usual, it was only an attempt to impress his father. You see, in addition to being a reverend, Mr. Caldwell was an avid horseman who had won many derbies. I had known of my friend's wish to follow in his footsteps for as long as I could remember.

As I glanced at him, I recalled all the times he had gotten me into trouble because of his pitiful obsession with Miss Hoffman. "Meet you at the finish line!" I called, as I picked up the pace and galloped off in a cloud of dust. I rode and rode until I had the finish line in my sight. I rode through just as Matthew came up behind me. The crowd cheered as we both came to a halt.

"Show off!" Matthew exclaimed angrily and went into a coughing fit.

I grinned slightly, "Perhaps, if you got your head out of the clouds, you could beat me for a change."

"Well done boys," our fathers congratulated us, coming forward from the crowd.

"I could have made it first, had Jonathan not left me trailing in a cloud of dust!" Matthew raged.

My father shook his head, "Must you two take it so seriously? It is not a professional competition."

"Forgive me, Father," I apologized, regaining my composure. "We do tend to get a bit carried away at times."

"You will need to be less reckless in the future, if you ever wish to join the professionals. You would both be disqualified for a stunt like that," Mr. Caldwell scolded.

"Yes, Father," Matthew replied, as he dismounted and sulked off.

With a sigh, I dismounted as well and followed after him, "Matthew, your father is only trying to help you."

"He would not have had to help me if you had not left me trailing in the wind!" he fumed.

"Calm down."

"No!" he roared.

I looked around, desperately trying to find something with which to distract him. Then I spotted her. "Look, Miss Hoffman is here," I told him.

He stopped dead in his tracks. "Where?" he asked.

"She is just ahead of us, speaking with Miss Abbott," I explained, pointing her out to him.

"What should I say?" he panicked.

I rolled my eyes, "You are asking the wrong man."

"Fine, I shall think of something myself," he said, as he gathered up his courage and walked up to them. I followed.

"Miss Abbott," he greeted. "Miss Hoffman."

"Mr. Caldwell," Louise acknowledged us. "Mr. Gilmore."

I did not know Louise Abbott very well, but I did know that she was vain and incredibly rude. She also happened to be courting Matthew's younger brother, James. I viewed them to be a near-perfect match, due to their similar personalities. For a moment, I found myself wondering why anyone would care to tolerate either of them.

"Are you enjoying the derby?" Matthew asked politely.

"What is not to enjoy? The sun is shining, the wind is fairly calm, and the riders seem to be in such good spirits! Surely the Lord has blessed this event!" she exclaimed.

"I am glad that you find the weather to your liking," he said with a smile. "Did you happen to catch our last race?"

She nodded her head. "You both ride uncommonly fast. For a moment, I thought it was going to end in a tie."

"Do you ride, yourself?"

"I do adore a good trail ride; however, I could never ride in a derby like this."

"Do you ride, Miss Hoffman?"

"I am afraid that I do not," Miss Hoffman replied, as she glanced about as if looking for someone. "You will have to excuse me. I believe my father is looking for me."

"You said that you would allow me to introduce you to a few people!" Miss Abbott attempted to stop her.

"You may introduce me to them later. I must go see what my father needs for now." With that she took her leave.

Miss Abbott appeared to be annoyed at that. "By any chance, do you happen to know if your brother is competing in the derby?" she asked.

"I believe he is going to be riding quite soon actually."

"Then I must go wish him luck," she said eagerly, as she rushed off towards the stables.

Mathew looked off in the direction Miss Hoffman had departed. "There goes my second chance," he sulked.

"I am still not convinced that she is the right woman for you."

"This coming from a man who does not even believe in love," he retorted.

"While I may not believe in it, I am not convinced that opinions should be based on appearance or wealth," I explained, "and besides, you barely know her."

"I have known her since the age of six," he defended.

"That is not what I meant," I corrected him. "What is she interested in? Do you even know her favourite colour?"

He sighed, "I suppose that you are correct, but how am I to learn her interests if we never get the chance to speak?"

"Well, you have just learned that she does not ride."

"Surely you must know something about her."

"How would I know anything about her? In case you have not noticed, I've barely spoken two words to her in my entire life."

"Your sister teaches her music lessons. Perhaps she has mentioned something."

"I am not particularly close to my sister. I would not know even if she *had* mentioned something."

"Have you seen her in music lessons before?"

"No."

"Have you ever seen her in your house?"

"No," I repeated. "I am not the type of man to take interest in every woman who enters my house."

"Your brother is right; you really are a wall-flower."

"Spare me your insults. If it makes you feel any better, I shall try to pay closer attention when Miss Hoffman has her music lessons."

"Perhaps you could ask your sister about her sometime."

"I am most certainly not going to ask anyone about her. If I do, they will begin to question my motives, and then I will have to inform them of your obsession over her."

He turned bright red with embarrassment. "What can I say? She is very beautiful."

He certainly did have a point there. Even I had to admit that she was indeed very beautiful, with her bright blue eyes and long blonde hair. However, I was still convinced that the only reason my friend adored her was for her beauty. He knew nothing of her character.

"I cannot help but think that you adore her for her appearance alone."

"I assure you it is not so. Besides, what do you know of love? You would not even know it if you were in it."

"Must you mock me?" I asked in an irritated tone.

"Forgive me, but I do not believe you should be lecturing me on love when you have not even noticed a woman let alone loved one."

"I have noticed many young ladies; however, I am hardly interested in any of the women who follow me around relentlessly."

"If that is the case, you will end up either alone for your entire life or forced into an arranged marriage like your brother."

Truth be told, I could well enough imagine myself being forced into an arranged marriage. Although I found the idea completely repulsive, it was the only path I could see in front of me. In my mind, love was nothing but a mirage, and marriage consisted of nothing but misery and toleration.

CHAPTER FOUR

Life seemed bleak to me as I sat in front of the window in Louise's bedroom. I had arrived at the Abbotts' estate for a regular visit earlier in the afternoon in hopes of having a pleasant conversation for once, but sadly that was not the case. Louise had been complaining about how I had left her and broken my promise. After a while, I had lost interest in listening to her ramblings and had resorted to watching a spider crawl along the window pane.

"You promised that you would allow me to introduce you to three of the contestants! The only men that we talked to were Matthew Caldwell and Jonathan Gilmore!" she rambled. "Helene, are you even listening to me?"

"I am listening, Louise," I said with a sigh, as I turned to face her. "I am sorry, but my father was looking for me."

"Your father is always looking for you!" she exclaimed. "How does he expect you to ever get married if he does not allow you to meet anyone?"

In complete honesty, my father rarely ever called me to him. I prayed that God would forgive me, but I normally used that as an excuse to get away from Matthew Caldwell and his friend. I could understand if he wished to get to know me a bit better, but I dearly wished he would see that I was simply not interested in him. I also wished that Louise would see that I really could not have cared less about getting married. Do not misunderstand, I have seen many men whom I find more or less desirable. The only problem was that most of them were arrogant and selfish.

"I am unsure of that myself," I said, hoping to convince her that I did have a slight hope for marriage.

"Perhaps I should have James arrange a meeting for you and his elder brother. Matthew Caldwell is a fine gentleman."

I shivered at the thought, "I doubt that James would do such a thing for me. He is not the most fond of me."

"You may be right," she pondered over the issue. "What about Jonathan Gilmore? Is he not the most handsome man you have ever laid eyes on?"

"Jonathan Gilmore?" I let out a small giggle. "I must admit that both he and his elder brother are very handsome; however, I do not believe that would work either. He is a nobleman after all."

"That is true. I imagine that he is already engaged to a different woman. You know how society is."

Louise was quite correct. In high society, it seemed that a family's goal was to marry their children off to whomever they felt would help them increase their wealth and rank. In my own life, our goal was to keep the family alive. Everything out here was so different from what I was originally accustomed to.

Since my arrival, nearly thirteen years ago, I had worked feverishly to master the English language, as well as England's customs and etiquette. There had been many times that I would have liked to give up and return to our homeland, but deep down I knew that it was unlikely to happen. It seemed that we were destined to spend the rest of our lives stuck in England. So I understood her point.

"I have noticed that," I replied, deep in thought.

I had to admit that the thought of Jonathan Gilmore being engaged had never crossed my mind. It certainly had not seemed that way when Caroline had spoken to me of him. I quickly shook that thought from my mind and went back to concentrating on Louise. Why should I care whether he was engaged or not.

"Whomever he marries will be a fortunate woman," Louise said. "She will have a desirable husband and an extremely large fortune," she sighed, "everything that a woman could possibly want."

I rolled my eyes as I averted them to the window once again. Then, rather suddenly, I noticed a carriage coming up the road. "It appears that you have more guests."

"I completely forgot to tell you! My parents invited the Caldwells over for dinner," she explained.

"What?!" I exclaimed. My world had come crashing down on me in the blink of an eye. There was no way that I could avoid him until my father came to pick me up after dinner. I was doomed to a never-ending evening of being uncomfortable.

"Since you are here, now would be a good opportunity for you to get to know Matthew Caldwell. Maybe one day we will be sisters," she giggled with delight, as she rushed out of the room.

"I need to find a better friend," I mumbled to myself, as I whispered a quick prayer and followed after her.

"Hurry up, Helene!" she exclaimed, racing down the stairs and to the front door.

Louise always seemed to get excited whenever James was around. Personally, I could not see what was so exciting about him. He happened to be nothing more than a selfish, mean-spirited boy who was quite fond of Louise.

"It is good to see you again, Harold," Mr. Caldwell said, greeting Mr. Abbott.

"Helene, come out and greet the Caldwells!" she exclaimed, pulling me out onto the front porch.

"I am coming," I assured her. Out of the corner of my eye, I could see how Matthew's eyes widened when he saw me. I suppose that he had not expected to see me either. How I wished that I had come a day later.

"Miss Hoffman, it is nice to see you again," Mrs. Caldwell greeted me with a tender smile.

"It is nice to see you all as well."

As we escorted them into the dining room, I could hear Mrs. Caldwell and Mrs. Abbott whispering behind me. "Such a polite young lady," I heard one of them say. "It is no wonder your daughter is so fond of her."

"That is not the reason she is fond of me," I muttered under my breath.

"Miss Hoffman," Matthew called, as he walked up beside me. "Are you staying for dinner?"

"It is indeed my intention," I answered, trying my hardest to be polite.

He continued his questioning. "Do you visit the Abbotts often?"

"I do occasionally visit them," I replied, as we arrived in the dining room. I attempted to sit as far away from him as possible, but my attempt failed miserably. I found myself trapped between James Caldwell and Mrs. Abbott, and across from Matthew.

"Reverend, would you bless the food?" Mr. Abbott asked.

"Of course," Mr. Caldwell replied, as he folded his hands and closed his eyes. "Sovereign Lord, we give thanks for this opportunity to gather with our friends. We give thanks for the food you have put before us, and may you bless the hands that have prepared it. In your holy name we pray, Amen."

"Amen," everyone echoed, as all at once the room began to erupt with chatter. Trays filled with meat, cheese, and vegetables were set out on the table along with teas of every blend. I recall thinking that there was enough food to feed an army. Although, the way that Matthew and Mr. Caldwell ate, you would think we had about twenty starving men in the room.

"How are your music lessons faring, Miss Hoffman?" Mrs. Caldwell asked.

"I should say that they are going quite well. Miss Caroline Gilmore is an excellent teacher," I replied with a smile.

"Yes, it is a pity that she wastes her good looks. She does resemble her mother quite beautifully," Mrs. Abbott complained.

"I must admit that she does; however, I am quite certain that she could still find a husband if she wished," Mrs. Caldwell defended.

"Do you like music, Miss Hoffman?" Matthew asked from across the table.

"I am indeed quite fond of music."

"Of course, she is not quite as talented as me," Louise boasted. "Miss Gilmore says that I am one of her best pupils."

"My Louise does seem to have a special talent for music," Mrs. Abbott joined in.

It was at that moment that I began to feel uncomfortable. This was the issue with having Louise as a friend. Whenever we were in the presence of important, high-society people, she would brag about how she was better than me at everything. It tended to make me feel as if it were true.

I had confronted her about it once before, but she had just laughed about it and assured me that she was only joking. I sighed. To me, friendship and marriage consisted of nothing more than toleration and pure misery. I could see nothing else in it.

"Will you need a ride home, Miss Hoffman? I could have the carriage prepared," Mr. Abbott offered.

"That is all right. My father will be coming right after dinner."

"Are you not coming fishing with us?" young Mary Caldwell asked. "We often go over to the pond after dinner."

"I am not fond of fishing. Besides, I do not think that I shall have the time to go with you."

While we finished our food, I occasionally caught the two families glancing over at me as if I had just said something appalling. By the time dinner was over, I was more than eager to leave. I would certainly have to ask whether they were expecting more guests next time, if indeed there were a next time.

CHAPTER FIVE

As I stepped out of the car-
riage, I was nearly ambushed by my friend, who seemed a bit too
eager about something. He had sent word for me to visit him, so that
he could discuss something with me. Originally I had not planned
on coming; however, I knew very well that he would end up at my
doorstep unannounced if I did not.

"What is it that you wanted to discuss with me?" I asked.

"Come down to the pond with me and I will tell you," he said
with a cheeky grin, as he ran off towards the fishing pond. With a
reluctant sigh, I started after him. He ran to the very edge before
sitting down on the grass. "Sit down."

"If you have dragged me all the way out here just to fish, I
will leave."

"I did not bring you here to fish," he assured me. "I brought you
here so that we may discuss Miss Hoffman further."

"I do not want to argue with you right now," I warned. "However,
if that is all that you wanted, I will be taking my leave now."

As I turned to go, he grabbed my arm to pull me back, "Wait! I
took your advice and got to know her better."

"When did you do that?" I asked, turning around to face him.
"We have not seen her since the derby."

"She happened to be visiting the Abbotts yesterday as well. I actually had a chance to talk to her during dinner," he explained.

"What did you all learn?"

"I learned that she likes tea, she is not fond of fishing, she adores music, and I believe she is quite fond of your sister."

At that moment, I felt like strangling him. "You have learned nothing," I groaned. "I have yet to meet a woman who does not like tea. If anything this just proves my point further. You would not be happy with her."

"Why not?" he persisted.

"You still know very little about her. Simply knowing whether or not she likes fishing is not enough to judge her character. For all you know she could be from a long line of terrorists."

"I am quite certain that she is not. Although, the way her father carries on he just may be a terrorist. He is constantly calling her away just when I get the chance to speak with her."

"Perhaps he does not like you," I suggested. "Bear in mind that you would have to tolerate him if you were ever to court her." I shuddered at the thought of any man or woman having to tolerate him. He always seemed to be grumpy about something. I had to say that it made me wonder about his reason for such behaviour.

"My father says that marriage is all about loving your wife and learning to accept her as well as her parents."

At that moment, I was certain that my eyeballs would pop out of their sockets. "Please do not say what I think you are going to say."

"I am planning on asking for her hand in marriage."

"What makes you think that she would want to marry you?" I asked, trying to control my frustration. "You have not even asked to court her."

"I see no reason why she would not accept," he replied. "Why are you so against it?"

"I simply do not want you to embarrass yourself. There is always the possibility that she will say no."

"You do not need to worry about me, Jonathan. She was very nice when I visited with her yesterday. Surely she would never wish to embarrass me."

Do not misunderstand my intentions, for I did very much want my closest friend to be happy; however, I still believed that he was blinded by her beauty. Perhaps I was so against it because I felt as though she might still be carrying a grudge against him.

Despite the fact that I had assured him otherwise, I was actually quite certain that she had been disappearing on purpose, which only encouraged him to pursue her. Whether this was done as a cruel joke or not, I could not know. The one thing that I did know was that I did not want my friend to have his heart broken.

"Are you certain that this is what you want? Do you realize that you may have to give up some things?"

"I really do not see why I would have to give up anything. I could still go riding and fishing, just not with her."

"I give up on trying to warn you," I sighed. "When will this proposal be taking place?"

"I was planning on doing it at your family's upcoming ball."

I could feel all the colour drain out of my face. The ball that he spoke of was to welcome a group of officers that would be arriving next month. I could already picture the scene that would take place. I could almost hear the crowd whispering behind his back as she refused him. "I beg that you reconsider."

"When else will I have the chance to speak with her?" he asked.

I racked my brain, trying to think of some other time that would be less humiliating for him. Then it hit me. "Has your father not invited the Hoffmans to the dinner party he's hosting a week before my family's ball?"

"That is a good idea. I could ask her then," he replied with a smile. "How should I go about asking her though?"

"How on earth would I know that? The only thing I advise is that you do it privately."

"All right, I shall try to do it in private," he assured me. "Will you be there as well?"

"I will most likely be lurking about in the shadows, making sure that you do not ask her in the middle of the meeting."

"In which room should I ask her?"

"I could not care any less. As long as it is in a room where no one will hear or see you."

He contemplated how he would go about his proposal for a while before coming to a conclusion. "Everyone will be in the drawing room for a short period of time following dinner. I could propose to her outside in front of the fountain. Women do tend to like a romantic proposal."

"Do you really think that is wise? You may just end up pushing her into the fountain," I said cynically.

"Why would I do that?"

"You have been known to be rather dangerous when you are angry." I looked at him sternly and he seemed to understand what I meant.

"She is not going to say no," he sighed. "Perhaps the music room is a better option, though. She is fond of music."

"At least no one will be able to hear you scream from there."

"Why would I scream?"

"You will when you kick the piano in a fit of rage."

He rolled his eyes at me. "I am capable of controlling my temper, Jonathan."

"Of course you are. Kicking that rock in the Seymour manor garden was a good illustration of that."

"Why must you always make fun of me?"

"It is entertaining to me," I teased. "If you really do insist on asking for Miss Hoffman's hand in marriage, I only ask that you consider what you will have to give up and try to prepare yourself in case she does say no."

"Of course I am going to think about it," he assured me, as he looked up at the sky. "Although, to be honest with you, I believe that I will be absolutely fine."

As I watched him, I could not help but feel that he was only telling me this in order to put a stop to my lectures. I prayed to God, begging him to take pity on my friend and spare him a broken heart. I then tried to convince myself that everything would turn out all right in the end. Perhaps Miss Hoffman really would accept his proposal. Surely everything would go according to God's ultimate plan, whatever that may be.

CHAPTER SIX

In all my life, I had never
found a single family that I dreaded visiting more than the Caldwells.
While I was quite fond of Mr. Joseph Caldwell as a reverend, I
dreaded visits such as these for the very presence of his two sons.
Although, I had actually visited the Caldwell manor quite a few
times over the years, I could never help but get nervous when entering the house of horrors.

You may ask why I would call it that, but I assure you that I had
a good reason. There were so many painful memories linked to that
house, which I could not seem to forget about no matter how hard I
tried. I could easily recall a particular event that had ended in much
pain. We had been playing a game of blind man's bluff when James
decided to surprise me by throwing a rock at my head, hitting me in
the mouth. It had started bleeding so much that my parents took me
home immediately. I believe that was when I first began to think of
it as a house of horrors.

As I made my way into the dining room, I was greeted by a room
filled with happy chattering guests. Fortunately, Matthew and his
friend Jonathan Gilmore were seated at the other side of the table.
Unfortunately, I ended up being seated between Louise and Vincent
Gilmore. *"Surely it could not be any worse than the time at the Abbotts'
house,"* I thought. I did not realize just how wrong I was.

During dinner, Louise whispered suggestions to me in one of her many attempts to find a suitable match for me. "Mr. Butler would be a fine choice. His father does own a rather large industry."

"I would prefer someone who is a Christian," I replied, taking a sip of my soup.

"What about Mr. Black? He happens to be very wealthy," she suggested.

"He also happens to be forty-five years old and a widower," I retorted.

"What about Mr. Jenkins?"

"He may be desirable in appearance, but when it comes to personality, I must say that he is almost as rude as Jonathan Gilmore," I whispered in Louise's ear, to ensure that the elder Gilmore brother would not hear me.

"You are quite right in that aspect," she agreed with a slight giggle. "How about Mr. Connell? He is handsome, polite, and only twenty-one years old. That is only two years past your own age."

"Louise, can we please continue this discussion later?" I requested. "I would prefer to finish my soup."

"Fine," she agreed. "I shall not be deterred from this topic, however."

After dinner had ended and everyone had arrived in the drawing room for the meeting, Louise pulled me into a corner of the room to further our discussion, "Now, what is wrong with Mr. Connell?" she asked.

"I will admit that his face is appealing, but you are forgetting that he is already married."

"I had forgotten about that," she admitted. "Dr. Weston is a fine doctor and would suit you very well."

"I hear that he is more devoted to his practise than to finding a wife."

"That is the problem with these men. They are all either married or uninterested," she complained.

"Why have you not mentioned Mr. Wilcox?" I asked. "He is a very nice man."

"His nose is enormous and crooked. Why on earth would you want to marry him?"

"Not everyone judges people on their appearances. I would prefer to marry someone who will not make my life miserable at the very least."

She pretended to ignore my last words, "Can you imagine the men we would meet if we lived in London? We would go to the most amazing balls and dance the entire night with officers and nobility!"

While Louise carried on with her unrealistic fantasies, I noticed Jonathan Gilmore slip out the door, leaving his friend on the opposite side of the room. I could tell that he was watching me closely, as if he thought I would disappear into a puff of smoke at any moment. Without a doubt, he was preparing himself to come talk to me again.

"What are you looking at?" Louise asked.

"Nothing," I lied. "I was only admiring the painting on the wall over there. Do you happen to know who painted it?"

"I have no such idea. I am afraid that I do not take much interest in art," she replied.

As I turned to go join the meeting, I was cut short by Matthew Caldwell. "It was painted by an artist in London as a gift for my father," he explained.

"Mr. Caldwell!" Louise exclaimed with surprise. "We had not seen you there."

"Forgive me for startling you," he apologized. "Are you enjoying yourselves?"

"Of course, it is always an immense delight to visit your home."

"Delight" was not the word that I would have used to describe my visits. A more suitable word might have been "mistake" or "nightmare". I was certain that Louise was only being nice to him because of his fortune and family connections, just like any other society woman would.

"I wonder if I may speak with Miss Hoffman alone for a moment," he asked nervously.

"Of course you may," she winked at me, as she hurried off towards where James was seated.

I tried to think of a logical explanation for his wanting to speak with me alone. While I could well enough understand it if he were trying to get to know me better, I still wished that he would realize that I was not interested in him and just leave me alone.

"Perhaps, we had best go into the music room where we shall not be disturbed," he suggested.

"Very well," I agreed with hesitation. He escorted me into the music room at the other side of the house, where he then began to close the doors. As he did so, I began to grow more and more suspicious. What on earth was he up to?

He then turned to face me, "I am quite certain that by now you have taken notice of my feelings towards you."

I held my breath as his words sunk in. Had he brought me into the music room to profess his feelings for me or was there some other reason? I could not help but feel that I should have declined his request to speak with me privately.

"I must inform you that I have loved you for quite a few years," he continued. "I have struggled to keep my feelings hidden; however, I can bear it no longer."

My eyes widened as I finally realized why he had brought me here. Surely he could not be so ignorant of my efforts to get away from him. He could not possibly mean what I thought he did.

"I must ask you," he said with a slight pause. "Would you do me the honour of becoming my wife?"

I stood there in a state of utter shock. I could not believe my ears. Matthew Caldwell had just asked for my hand in marriage. The very man who had mocked and teased me relentlessly as a child now wanted to marry me! I had forgiven him for that a long time ago, of course, but I found myself believing his so-called feelings were based on regret.

I had to admit that it chilled me to the bone just thinking about a life spent with him. By accepting his offer, I would be throwing away my own happiness in order to please him for a little while. Who knows if it would even last? There was one thing that I did know: A life spent with Matthew Caldwell would be a very unpleasant one.

After considering my reply very carefully, I decided that it would be best to put an end to this once and for all, "I am afraid that I do not return your feelings. That being the case, I must say that I cannot bring myself to accept your offer."

As I studied his facial expression, I saw at first nothing but humiliation and sadness. Then I spotted a bit of anger. Without a moment's thought, I rushed out of the room in fear of his temper. I should have gone back into the drawing room and pretended that nothing had happened, but for some reason I felt compelled to stay and find out what would happen next.

I lingered a short distance down the hallway, and heard someone enter the room. Somehow I knew that it was Jonathan Gilmore, who had most likely been eavesdropping the whole time. "I am such a fool," Matthew said bitterly. "You tried to warn me and I did not listen."

"There was no way for you to know that she would reject you," Jonathan replied.

He was silent for many moments before speaking again. "You were right, Jonathan. She most likely put me through all of this as revenge for how I treated her as a child."

At that moment, it felt like someone had just ripped my heart out. *"Jonathan Gilmore told his friend that I have done this as revenge?"* I questioned in disbelief. *"What have I even done?"*

All of the respect I'd ever had for him disappeared like smoke. Surely he was the one who was cruel if he had convinced his friend of this. I knew for a fact that he'd been aware of my many attempts to escape his friend and I feared that he also knew about the lies I told Matthew and Louise about my father calling for me.

Surely I had done nothing to encourage Matthew Caldwell's feelings for me.

I wondered about his reason behind this. Had he really believed that I wished for revenge or was that a lie as well? Had he convinced Matthew of this in order to make him hate me? Certainly his best friend would know that he was prone to act appallingly when angered. *"Perhaps it is his intention to disgrace me and my family,"* I thought. And with that, I decided that I had heard enough and rushed off to rejoin the meeting.

CHAPTER SEVEN

A week had passed, and once again I found myself staring at the endless number of couples as they danced. However, it was not the couples on whom I was focusing tonight. Instead, I was focused on my friend's situation. He had been heartbroken and humiliated by Miss Hoffman, whom I had begun to think of as a selfish and cruel person.

The only thing that I was thankful for was that no one had seemed to notice Matthew disappear. If we could keep it a secret, surely everything would end well. Although, I could not help but think that Miss Hoffman had intentions of disgracing him.

He had been a fool, but I still felt sorry for him. In my eyes, Miss Hoffman had seemed cruel and without regret in her actions. Obviously Matthew had been mistaken when he said that she was very polite, because in her delivery of the rejection she seemed quite the opposite to me.

"Do you refuse to dance even at a ball hosted by your own family?" Vincent asked, coming up to me.

"I have told you many a times before that I do not enjoy dancing," I replied.

"Well, could you possibly put your own desires aside and dance this one time? Mother keeps nagging me to come talk to you," he complained, "and it is starting to get annoying, considering that it takes me away from my own enjoyment."

"Then return to your petty amusements. I am afraid that you are wasting your time with me."

"All right, be a gloomy Gus." He let out an irritated sigh and returned to his dancing partner.

As I turned my attention toward Miss Hoffman, who was speaking with her sister-in-law, Charlotte, near the entrance, I began to wonder what exactly had been her reasoning for such a cruel rejection. I had already suspected that she may not return Matthew's feelings; however, that did not justify her actions. She could have gone about it differently. She could have let him down more gently.

There was a part of me that wanted to question her motives, and yet there was also a part of me that wanted to cling to the idea that she was cold-hearted. After battling with my conscience for many moments, I finally decided that I would do the unthinkable. I would ask her to dance with me, but only to question her. Even though I fully expected her to decline me just as she had Matthew.

Slowly I made my way over to where she was standing, and asked something that I never thought I would. "Miss Hoffman, might I have this next dance?" I asked her solemnly.

At first she appeared to be quite surprised; however, her expression hardened shortly after. "You may," she replied.

I escorted her to the centre of the ballroom, where the other couples stood waiting for the next dance to begin. As the music started and everyone began to dance, I noticed that all the eyes in the room were on me. They were most likely shocked to see that I was actually dancing for a change. I only hoped that this would eliminate the complaints made by my family as well. "I am rather surprised that you accepted my invitation," I commented.

"I did so because I know your reasoning behind offering it," she claimed.

"Do you really?" I wondered. "Please, do enlighten me."

"I am not one of those silly, empty-headed girls who dr
dancing with you, Mr. Gilmore. The only reason you asked 1
dance is so that you may question me," she declared.

"And what is it that I wish to question you about?" I tested her.

"Without a doubt, you wish to question my motives regarding a certain event that occurred last week. One that involved your closest friend," she replied quietly. "Although, I am surprised that he is not here asking me himself."

"He has been feeling poorly since the event I am afraid," I informed her. "Not that you would care."

"Ask me what you want so that we may go back to our separate parts of the world."

"Was it your intention to humiliate him as a cruel joke?" I asked.

"It was not my intention to come off as cruel. If it is the way he treated me as a child that convinces you otherwise, you may rest assured that I do not hold that against him any longer. I forgave him for that quite some time ago."

"If revenge is not the case, then what were your motives?"

"It is my turn to ask you a question now, Mr. Gilmore," she interrupted.

"What do you want to know?"

"I want to know your own motives behind this. From what I have heard, you had your friend convinced that I was a selfish and cruel person."

"Where did you hear that?" I asked with surprise.

"I will admit that I overheard you and your friend speaking right after I left the room," she admitted. "If you despised me with such a passion, would you not attempt to disgrace me for my offence?"

I was taken back by her sudden accusation. "It has never been my intention to disgrace anyone," I assured her. "Now, back to the question I had asked you before you interrupted me: What were your motives? Certainly they were not driven by compassion."

"I do not take back what I said; however, I assure you that I did have logical reasons."

"In that case, would you care to state your reasons?"

"Are you certain that you wish to know?"

"I most certainly do."

"Very well," she hesitated briefly. "First of all, I could not see anything but misery in a life with him. Do you deny that your friend has a horrid temper? One that is known to erupt at the most minor of upsets?"

"I will admit that he does."

"Second of all, I am quite certain that you have taken notice of my many attempts to get away from him, and as you have probably heard, I do not feel the same way that he does."

"Indeed I have."

"Finally, did you ever consider that perhaps I am not the type of woman to even believe in love?" She stated her last reason just as the dance ended.

My eyes widened in shock. For the first time, I could actually understand her actions. Everything that she had said was because she did not believe in love, and in all honesty, I could not say that I blamed her.

"I am sorry to hear that your friend is not well at the moment, and I am sorry if I have wounded his ego severely; however, I simply could not bring myself to accept his most horrible and ignorant offer." And with that, she excused herself and went her separate way.

While I made my way back to my previous position, I pondered over our argument. Had I really misunderstood her motives so much by thinking her a seeker of revenge? Had she really thought that I would use it against her, in order to avenge my friend? One thing was for certain though: All of the anger I had felt just a few minutes prior had completely disappeared.

I was curious as to why a woman with such a beautiful face and figure would share my views on love. Perhaps I really had thought that I was the only one who felt this way. As I thought about her, it crossed my mind that Matthew would most likely question whether I had discovered anything about her from our exchange.

I contemplated whether or not I should inform him of her reasoning. While it may make him feel less foolish, I highly doubted that Miss Hoffman would appreciate it if I told him what she had shared in confidence. I hated the thought of having to lie to him, but felt that it might be necessary.

Perhaps I would have to speak with her further. I had no clue how or when I would manage to do so, but for some odd reason, I was curious to learn the depths of her disbelief in love and compare them to my own.

"I hear that you finally tried your hand at dancing," Vincent said with a grin, as he came towards me. "Who was the lucky woman?"

"How should I know?" I lied.

"You mean to tell me that you did not even learn her name?" he asked in astonishment.

"I selected a young lady at random because I was becoming tired of you pestering me constantly."

He sighed, "You probably did not even notice the colour of her hair."

I glanced briefly at Miss Hoffman and then back at my brother. "It was blonde."

"I beg your pardon?"

"Her hair was blonde," I repeated, as I started out of the ballroom.

"Well, that hardly provides me with any clues. There are dozens of blonde women in the room," he complained, following after me. "Why must you always act like such a know it all?"

"Why must you always act like the town flirt?" I retorted.

"Since when am I the town flirt?"

I rolled my eyes. "Face it, Vincent, you are very much a flirt."

"I most certainly am not!" he argued.

"Then why is it that you have danced with every woman in the room?"

"I will have you know that there are quite a few girls with whom I have not danced!"

"Given enough time, you will dance with them as well," I concluded, as I swung open the library door and slammed it shut behind me.

"Gloomy Gus," he grumbled.

CHAPTER EIGHT

In the past, I had always enjoyed my visits to the Gilmore manor; however, today I felt slightly unnerved. I could still see Jonathan Gilmore's face in my mind. I suppose that he had not expected me to say what I did. Of course, it would get uncomfortable being in the same room together from now on, but when had it not been uncomfortable for me? My feelings had needed to be made clear to him, and now that they were, I felt much more free.

While I was escorted to the second floor by the butler, I began to replay our heated argument, which had taken place a couple of nights prior. It would seem that both of us had misunderstood the other. He had thought that I was going to disgrace Matthew, and I thought that he was going to disgrace me.

So many questions danced around in my head. Could it be that he was listening in to ensure that his friend's anger did not destroy the house? Why would he go out of his way just to confront me? Did he really care that much about his friend? He certainly did not seem to be the type.

His invitation had certainly drawn the attention of the young ladies at the ball. Louise had begged me for details when she learned that Jonathan Gilmore had asked me to dance. Once I told her that he had only asked me in order to silence the complaints made by his peers, she seemed to calm down. At the very least, I was assured that she would not start a ridiculous rumour about him being enamoured with me.

"I trust that you will be able to find your way to the music room," the butler said, as we reached the landing.

"Of course," I said with a nod, before making my way down the corridor. While walking, I studied the many paintings and portraits that lined the walls. There was one of the Governor posed on a magnificent white horse, and another of the entire family in the garden. Mr. Gilmore and his wife were seated in the centre with a twelve-year-old Caroline, ten-year-old Vincent, and eight-year-old Jonathan surrounding them. By his appearance in the painting, it seemed that even as a child Jonathan was rather distant towards the others.

When I arrived at the music room, I found that the door was already open. Inside Caroline was seated on a sofa drinking a cup of tea. "Helene!" Her face brightened when she noticed me. "Come in and let us begin our lesson."

"Very well," I agreed, taking a seat in front of the piano. "Where is Louise? Normally she is still in lessons at this time."

"Her family had a previous engagement to attend to," she explained, coming to stand at my side. "Would you care to demonstrate for me how you have been faring with the song I gave you last week?"

"Of course," I replied, beginning to play. One thing that I enjoyed in England was having the chance to learn about the many famous composers and poets. I could play quite a few compositions, yet I still strove to learn more. One of my favourite composers happened to be Mr. Johann Sebastian Bach. His compositions inspired me to do my best and expect nothing more. All of my worries seemed to fade away whenever I heard his music.

A servant then entered the room. "Miss Caroline, your mother has requested that you join her in the parlour for tea."

She sighed. "You may tell her that I will join her in a minute."

"As you wish." The servant nodded and took her leave.

"You may try one of Mr. Bach's compositions while I am gone. I know how eager you are to learn his music."

I smiled, "I will give it a try."

"And I will try to be back before the end of the lesson," she told me, before rushing out of the room.

I flipped the papers towards one of Mr. Bach's more well-known compositions and began to play. While I played, I thought of my childhood in Germany. Memories of running around with my beloved elder brother flooded my mind. It was at moments like these that I could forget about all the pain and sorrow I had ever felt in life, and be at peace with myself.

Then, as I came to the end of the song, I heard a sudden clapping. I spun my head around to find Jonathan Gilmore leaning against the door frame, as if he had been there all along. Surely I had gotten so caught up in my own little world that I had not even heard him come in.

"My sister has taught you well," he complimented.

"She is indeed an excellent teacher," I replied, turning around to face him. "Might I ask what you are doing here?"

"Am I not allowed to listen to you play the piano, Miss Hoffman?" he asked.

"You may do as you please; however, I hardly believe that you would come here just to listen to me."

"You are wiser than I had thought," he noted, coming to stand beside me.

"Wisdom is not required to notice the fact that I have never seen you in all my years of coming here."

"Are you always this observant?" he asked.

"It is difficult not to take notice in a house this large," I stated. "Now, if you would be so kind as to tell me what prompted such a visit?"

"I would like to continue our previous conversation."

"I have nothing more to say to you about that. The only thing I wish to know is whether you intend to keep this a secret."

"It has never been my intention to reveal this unfortunate event in any way. However, I suppose that I need not worry about you revealing it either."

"If I were to do that, I would be disgracing my own family."

"I-I do ... h-however," he stuttered with visible hesitation, "believe that I owe you an apology."

"Why is that?" I asked.

"It would seem that I have misunderstood you. I was convinced that you were selfish and cruel."

"I owe you an apology as well," I said in shame. "I have misunderstood you as well. I was convinced that you were nothing but an arrogant, proud peacock."

It was his turn to be surprised. "You thought that I was an arrogant, proud peacock?"

"I am not, by far, the only one who sees you in that way. I can name more than a dozen people who share this opinion."

"Dare I ask what the reasons behind this accusation are?"

"I believe it to be based upon your refusal to socialize at balls."

"I am sorry if it appears that way to others; however, that is because I am not comfortable among crowds. If I were to strike up a conversation with someone, I would get mobbed by a swarm of overly curious people."

"I can understand that." It would seem that Caroline had been correct about his refusal to socialize. He really was uncomfortable in crowds, just as I was. I was slowly beginning to see that we did have a bit in common with each other. Although I could not see enough to convince me that Caroline was entirely correct.

"There is one more thing that I am curious about, however."

"What is it?"

"At the ball, you briefly mentioned something about not believing in love."

My eyes widened. "Why would you be curious about such a thing?"

"I only wish to know if your disbelief matches my own."

I was quite surprised to learn that he did not believe in love either, though it would certainly explain his refusal to dance. "You do not believe in love?"

"That is correct."

"I will only tell you about my disbelief if you promise to never speak of it to another living soul."

"I would never do such a thing," he assured me.

I took a deep breath and began. "I do not believe that love between people can be real. I am convinced that marriage consists of nothing but toleration and misery," I explained. "When it comes to your friend's so-called affections, I am afraid to say that he bases his opinion of me on appearances and regret. He knows nothing about me, and I know nothing about him."

"I could not agree with you any more."

"Then I can assume that the true reason for your refusal to dance is based on this disbelief?"

"You seem to understand me quite well after all."

"Not at all. I am merely observing this from our conversation."

He smiled ever-so slightly before going to leave. "Forgive me for my interruption. I shall leave you to your music lesson."

"Wait," I said, getting up from the piano and walking towards him. "Before you leave, promise me again that you have no intention of using any of this against me in the future."

"You seem quite convinced that I am trying to disgrace you."

"When you find yourself in an unfamiliar country without a reliable friend to put your trust in, you tend to take such precautionary measures," I explained.

"I promise you that I will not use this against you, and I will not tell Matthew anything about this."

"Thank you," I mumbled as he left.

With a sigh of relief, I sat back down at the piano and began to play again. "It would seem that I really have misunderstood his character," I said to myself. He had also seemed calmer than when last we spoke. Perhaps it was just because my opinion of him had been changed quite suddenly, or because he was now more certain of my motives.

I was having trouble seeing how the most desirable man in town could not believe in love. Of course I could not blame him for it, but if word of this were to ever get out, there would certainly be a mob of angry and heartbroken women after him. Then again, I suppose that a similar scene would play out if Matthew were to ever learn my reasons.

"Helene?" Caroline called suddenly, snapping me out of my thoughts.

"Yes?" I asked.

"I have returned. Did you try one of Mr. Bach's compositions?"

"Actually, I did manage to play the Minuet in G Major."

"You learned the Minuet in G Major during the short period of time I was gone?" she asked in amazement.

"I will admit that I have been practising it at home."

"That is very good," she said, briefly looking at the clock on the end table. "It would seem that our music lesson has come to an end. I am sorry that I could not have been here sooner."

"Do not worry about it. When your parents call you to them, you drop everything and go," I said with a smile. "Besides, I happened to learn more than I expected."

She smiled back at me, "While we are on the topic of parents, I should add that yours are waiting for you. Your father in particular was quite anxious to leave."

"He is not fond of staying in one position for long periods of time. His limbs tend to stiffen if he does. In which case, I had better hurry before he decides to leave without me," I explained as I rushed out of the room.

"Goodbye!" she called.

What I had said earlier, about learning more than I had expected, was certainly true. I had not intended to learn that Jonathan Gilmore happened to share my opinion on love. Although it seemed hard to believe that a man like him would feel that way, I was secretly glad to know that I was not the only one.

CHAPTER NINE

If there was one place you could always find me, it was in the library. The library itself consisted of two full storeys jammed full of books. It was far from the best in England, but it was good enough for me. Nearly every book in existence, from William Shakespeare to Charles Dickens, could be found on its shelves.

In my own personal opinion, the library was more like a home to me than the rest of the manor, for I spent a great deal of my time browsing through its shelves. It seemed that each member of this household tended to stick to a certain part of the estate. Caroline tended to stay in the music room, teaching her students, and Vincent could normally be found out riding one of the many trails or shooting game birds. Father often remained in his study when he was at home, and Mother spent most of her time planning lavish garden parties and balls.

There were times when we could go several weeks without seeing one another. It was more common to pass a servant in the corridor than my mother or father. We were not particularly close, but that was simply what we had gotten used to growing up. My only wish was that I never had to see them.

"Jonathan, are you in here?" my mother called.

"Where else would I be?" I asked, not even bothering to look up from the book I was reading. "What do you want?"

"I wanted to inform you that I received a letter from my good friend Mrs. Bellinger, in Norwich," she explained, coming towards me. "She says that she will agree to an arranged marriage between you and her daughter, Luciana."

At the very mention of the words "arranged marriage," I slammed my book shut. "You may write her back, telling her that I am not interested."

"You have not even seen the girl, Jonathan. You may like her."

"I highly doubt that," I said, placing the book back on the shelf.

She was furious. "Why are you so against the idea of being married?"

"Why are you so insistent on marrying me off?" I asked out of turn.

"You know very well that it is your duty to marry well and continue the family name."

"That is Vincent's duty, not mine."

"As a member of the Gilmore family, you happen to share this duty with your brother and sister."

"It is not an obligation that we all feel the need to fulfil."

"I gave up on Caroline a long time ago. However, Vincent will marry without question and I expect you to do the same."

My mother had a way of pushing me to the point where I could no longer hide the way I felt. In normal cases that would have been good, but in this case it was far from it. "Caroline gets to choose her fate, but I do not?" I asked.

"Caroline chose against my wishes and her decision did not go without consequences," she said sternly. "Now I am going to write Mrs. Bellinger back, telling her that you would be delighted by the arrangement."

"If you do, I will deny her publicly," I warned.

"You would not dare!" she retorted. "You would be disgracing yourself!"

"If that is what it takes to get it through your thick skull, then so be it." I replied, rushing out of the library. I stormed down the corridor in rage. My only thought was to get out of this wretched place and go for a long walk. Whenever I felt angry or had something on my mind, I would go out for a walk. The fresh air had always helped to clear my head in the past.

I quickly grabbed my coat from the closet before yanking open the front door and heading out down the road. I breathed in the fresh morning air as if it were the first time I had done so. I was well aware that I had just threatened my own mother, but that seemed to be the only way to get it through to her. If anything, I had inherited my stubbornness from her. I may have said that my only option in life was an arranged marriage at one time, but when it came right down to it, I could not bring myself to go through with it. I simply could not see anything but misery in such a life.

Just then, a sudden thought dawned on me. Had Miss Hoffman not felt the same way when she refused Matthew? She had said that she could see nothing but misery in a life with him. For the first time, I fully understood her reason for refusing him.

I began to see just how similar we really were, despite coming from two completely different societies. Neither of us believed in love, and yet at the same time, neither of us wanted to end up in a life filled with misery. We were caught in the hopeless battle of life. However, I felt slightly relieved to know that there was someone who understood how I felt. For once in my life, there was someone to whom I could relate.

Matthew knew about my disbelief as well, but he tended to use it against me in arguments. It always worried me to think what would happen if he ever lost his temper and told the world by accident. I could just picture all of the heartbroken women who would be furious with me.

I suddenly heard a voice. "Jonathan Gilmore? What are you doing out here?"

I looked up to see Matthew and his father in their carriage, stopped before me. "I am just out on a walk, Mr. Caldwell," I said. "What brings you here?"

"I need to discuss something with your father. Is he at home?" Mr. Caldwell replied.

"I imagine that he is," I said, continuing on my walk.

"I will join you," Matthew announced, jumping out of the carriage.

"I will meet you up at the estate," Mr. Caldwell told his son before riding off.

Once his father was out of sight, Matthew began to hurry after me. "How far are you planning on walking?" he asked.

"I plan on walking until I get lost and possibly eaten alive by a wild animal," I muttered.

"Why on earth would you want to do that?" he asked.

"Forget about it," I sighed. "How have you been doing?"

"I am all right. I have been trying to pretend that nothing happened."

"Count your blessings, my friend. Imagine what would have happened if your nosey younger brother had followed you."

"That would have been a nightmare!" He shuddered at the thought. "Did you learn if ... if she had a good reason?"

I stopped in my tracks and considered what exactly to tell him about the situation. I had promised Miss Hoffman that I would keep it a secret, and yet I hated lying to my friend. It would seem that I was having to do a lot of things that I never thought I would because of the situation. "I have learned nothing," I lied.

"What was she like at the ball?" he questioned.

"She acted completely normal as far as I could tell."

"I guess she does still hold a grudge against me," he sulked.

"You should try to get over her and move on with your life," I suggested.

"How can I forget about her when I see her constantly? I will still see her in church, at balls, and every time my father calls a church council meeting."

"Speaking of your father, what did he want to discuss with my father?"

"He mentioned something about a graveyard," he said with a shrug. "That is all that I know."

"I suppose that I will find out eventually."

"Perhaps we should head back to your home, unless you were serious about getting eaten alive."

"I was only joking. As much as the thought tempts me, I would never try to get myself killed," I explained, starting back towards the manor.

"Why are you so gloomy?" he asked, following behind me, "I should be the one wanting to drop off the face of the earth."

"I had the pleasure of speaking with my mother today."

"That would explain it," he concluded. "Was it another lecture on your refusal to dance?"

"Surprisingly, she did not even mention it this time."

"Perhaps she has given up on it?"

"I highly doubt that."

"Are you ever going to dance with someone?"

"Only time will tell."

"I have never heard you say that before," he replied. "I thought you would have said something like, 'I will never dance with anyone!'" he exclaimed, trying his best to imitate my voice.

"Are you implying that I sound like Mr. Hoffman?" I asked.

He burst out laughing. "That was certainly not my intention."

Upon reaching the estate, we found Mr. Caldwell and my father standing outside. They appeared to be discussing something. "We shall see you tomorrow afternoon," Father said.

"Where are we going tomorrow?" Matthew asked.

"We are all heading over to the Hoffmans' for tea," Mr. Caldwell explained.

The colour drained out of Matthew's face. "We are going there just for tea?"

"As you boys well know, Mr. Hoffman is the grounds keeper for the church. We need to discuss some things with him in regards to the graveyard," my father explained. "We decided that we would use it as a chance to visit with them."

"Come along, Matthew," Mr. Caldwell called, as he climbed into the carriage.

"Good luck," I quickly whispered to him, as he climbed in after his father.

"Make sure to bring those documents along!" Father called.

As we watched them go, a question came to mind. "Have we ever visited the Hoffmans at their house?" I asked.

"I do not think we have," my father observed, "nor even seen the house in which they live."

"It shall be a learning experience then," I replied. I had to admit that I was quite curious to discover what kind of life Miss Hoffman lived and how different it was from my own.

CHAPTER TEN

1 giggled with glee as 1 ran among the fields of Germany. The sound of the bleating sheep rang in my ears and the wind blew through my hair. My fifteen-year-old brother caught up with me and scooped me into his strong arms.

I felt happier than ever before. It was as if the world was only filled with light; however, that quickly changed. Instantly, the light disappeared and was replaced by dark, gloomy clouds. "What is the matter?" I asked, as he set me down.

BANG! A gunshot was fired out of nowhere. I watched in horror as my beloved older brother collapsed to the ground, a puddle of blood developing around him. Then, just as I was about to scream, I heard a voice call my name. "Helene!" The voice seemed closer now. "Aunt Helene, wake up!"

I opened my weary eyes to find my precious, four-year-old niece towering over me. It had only been a dream. "Giselle, what are you doing here?" I asked, sitting up and rubbing my eyes.

"Papa asked me to come wake you," she explained.

That was when it all came back to me. "What time is it?" I asked, looking around for a clock, only to remember that I did not have one in my bedroom.

"Papa says that our guests could be here any minute," she replied in a sweet, innocent tone.

I sprang to my feet. "I slept past noon? Alexander was supposed to wake me up hours ago!"

"He did not want to disturb you."

I lifted Giselle off the bed and set her down in the doorway, "Go fetch Grandmama and tell her to come and help me dress!" She rushed off immediately. "At this rate I will be lucky to have my corset tied by the time they arrive!"

I began to rush about, putting on my stockings and shoes before grabbing my corset and beginning to fasten the laces behind my back. "Helene, do you need help?" my mother called.

"Yes, Mama," I replied.

She came in and went straight to the job. "You are very fortunate to be so thin. I believe you inherited that from your father," she said with a laugh. "You are both nothing but skin and bones."

I smiled and breathed in. "Who all is coming for tea?" I asked.

"I am not quite certain. Mr. Caldwell said that his children had planned on visiting the Abbotts for a fishing trip."

"I suppose that we will have to wait and see then."

"There you go," she said, as she finished lacing. Then she slipped the corset cover over. "Which dress are you going to wear?"

I dashed over to my wardrobe and flung open the doors. My family had enough money to afford a few privileges. A small selection of dresses was included. "I was planning on wearing my light blue dress," I said, as I grabbed it and a few thick petticoats.

My mother began to help me slip the petticoats and dress over my head. Then, as I was about to leave, she stopped me, "Are you going to style your hair?"

"I will leave it hanging for the day," I replied, as I quickly brushed my hair.

She sighed. "You had best head down to the dining room and find something to eat then."

"Yes, Mama," I agreed, rushing out of the room and down the stairs.

Upon entering the dining room, I was greeted by my brother, Alexander. "Good afternoon, sleepy head," he teased.

"Good afternoon, Alexander," I retorted. "I must thank you for waking me up four hours late."

"You looked peaceful," he chuckled. "Forgive me for not wanting to disturb my little sister."

"That peace only lasts for a minute when you suddenly realize that there are guests coming," I grumbled, grabbing an apple from the bowl of fruit on the table. "Where is Papa?" I asked.

Charlotte then entered the room, carrying my adorable, one-and-a-half-year-old nephew, Henry. "He is in the study," she notified me.

I nodded my head and made my way to my father's study, which was hidden behind the staircase. That was where I found my elderly father sitting at his desk, surrounded by stacks of papers and books. Surely if there was one thing that I inherited from him, it was my fondness of reading.

"Ich sehe dass Dornröschen ist aufgewacht," Father greeted me in German. The English translation of this would have been, "I see that Sleeping Beauty has awoken." Dornröschen, or Sleeping Beauty, was the nickname given to me by my father at an early age. He was never certain if I would sleep for a hundred years or just all day.

"Good afternoon, Papa," I smiled happily at him as I gave him a gentle hug. "What are you working on?"

"A list of ideas that I want to discuss with Mr. Caldwell and Mr. Gilmore," he explained. "The graveyard is in need of some improvements."

"If you want my opinion, I would suggest adding some flowers or shrubs. It would definitely make the place less depressing," I said, as I browsed through one of the many bookshelves that lined the dark wooden walls.

"Looking for another book to read?" he asked.

"Actually, I am looking for something with which to distract Giselle. If I can keep her occupied, she should not be able to pester our guests."

"Well, if all else fails, you have my permission to take her outside."

"I am sure that will please her."

"They are here!" Charlotte called out all of a sudden.

I bolted towards the window to see who all had come. Fortunately, I did not spot even one of the Caldwells' children. "Thank God," I said, "the Caldwells did not bring their children."

"You do not seem to have any complaints against the Gilmores," Father commented, coming up beside me.

"I understand them better than the Caldwells," I admitted. "I understand enough to know that Mr. Gilmore and his wife do not get along."

"The problem is that she has such high expectations. Mrs. Gilmore is the type of woman who wants to establish herself in a higher society."

"A higher society? Does she expect to become the Queen of England?"

Just then, there was a knock on the front door. "Alexander, will you get that for me?" Father asked.

"All right," he called, as he rushed out of the dining room.

"Alexander, it is good to see you again," Mr. Gilmore greeted him. "Where is your father?"

"He is just finishing up some paperwork," Alexander explained, as I heard Mother come down the stairs.

"You may hide in here for the afternoon if you wish," Father teased.

"I have no reason to hide," I replied, setting my apple down on the desk and following him out.

"Ah, there you are," Mr. Caldwell said.

"Shall we go into the parlour?" Father asked.

"Yes, let us get straight to business," Mr. Gilmore agreed.

As they were all about to head into the parlour to begin their discussion, Father accidentally hit his leg against the door frame. Alexander and I rushed over to help stabilize him as he let out a bloodcurdling scream.

"Papa, are you all right?" I worried.

He winced in pain as he regained stability. "I am fine!"

"Is everything all right?" Mr. Caldwell asked. "Shall I send for a doctor?"

"That will not be necessary," Father grumbled, as he jerked out of our grasp and limped over to his chair.

"Charlotte dear, send Miss Wilkins in with the tea," Alexander instructed his wife, as he followed everyone into the parlour and shut the door.

As soon as the excitement was over, I decided to go see what Giselle was doing in her bedroom. Technically, it had been Alexander's old bedroom, but since he had a house of his own now, we had decided to convert it into a guest room for when Giselle comes to stay with us.

I opened the last doorway on the left to find my beautiful niece seated on her bed, playing with one of my old dolls. She jumped off as soon as she saw me, "Is everyone all right? I thought I heard someone scream."

"Everyone is fine," I assured her. "Grandpapa just hit his bad leg. The guests are all settled in and I was wondering what you wanted to do."

She thought about it for a while. "Raid Grandpapa's study!" she exclaimed.

I grinned, "All right."

Within the blink of an eye, she had grabbed my hand and was hurrying me back down into the study. I picked up my apple again and took a large bite out of it before selecting a book from one of the piles.

"I found a book!" Giselle exclaimed proudly, holding up a thick, heavy book.

I let out a small laugh and sat down at Father's desk to read my book. Giselle settled down at my feet and began to flip through her own. After reading for no more than three minutes, Giselle grew tired of reading. Somehow I knew that she would not stay content for long. She was more like Alexander in that respect.

"This book makes no sense!" she exclaimed.

I put down my book and examined hers. "That is because it is written in German."

"What do we do now?" she asked.

"How about going for a walk," a familiar voice suggested.

I looked up to find Jonathan Gilmore standing in the doorway. I nodded to him. "I presume that you have grown tired of listening to my father."

"You could say that," he replied.

Giselle tugged at the hem of my dress. "Can we walk over to the stream?"

"I was given permission to take you outside. If our guest insists on going for a walk, then I suppose we can. However, you will need to put your shoes on first."

"Can I bring Lucy?" she asked, as she ran off.

"All right, but try not to drop her into the water this time," I called after her.

"Who is Lucy?"

"Her doll," I informed him, putting the books away and heading to the front door.

"I am ready!" she exclaimed, as she came rushing down the stairs, clutching an old, red-haired rag doll in her arms.

While we walked along the thin path that led to the stream, Giselle would stop to pick a flower for me or admire something out of the blue, and every so often I would sneak a quick glance at Jonathan, who seemed to be looking around at the scenery. "Might I ask what your reason is for wanting to join us on a walk?" I asked out of curiosity.

"It would seem that I always have to have a reason with you," he noted.

"I suppose that I am still accustomed to the man I thought you were," I admitted.

"I do not always have a reason, Miss Hoffman. There are times that I simply want to get away from my parents," he explained.

"I can certainly understand that. My own father can be quite unpleasant at times."

"Why is your father so unpleasant?" he asked.

I saddened slightly, "I am afraid to say that there are a couple of reasons."

"And they are?" he persisted.

"It all started about a year before we immigrated here. My oldest brother was killed."

"You had more than one brother?"

I nodded. "His name was Wilhelm."

"What happened to him?"

"He got mixed up in a terrorist outbreak. One of the officers mistook him for a terrorist and shot him dead. My father has never been the same since that day."

His eyes widened. "And the other reason?"

"A few months after Wilhelm's death, my father injured his leg. At first we did not think that it was serious; however, as time progressed, his leg got much worse. One morning he woke up in immense pain. We called for the doctor immediately, but it was soon evident that the wound had been left untended for too long. There was nothing that the doctor could do for him except to chop it off."

He was horrified. "He only has one leg?"

I nodded. "We managed to get him a wooden leg, but using it pains him quite a bit—especially if he hits it against something."

"That was why he screamed earlier," he concluded.

"I hope that you will keep this a secret as well."

He was silent for a moment. "Do you really trust me?"

"I am unsure of who I can trust in this world, but I do know things that would send an angry mob of women after you."

"That is an excellent point."

"Stream!" Giselle exclaimed happily as we approached the small river. It was not very deep, but it did have enough water to splash around in.

"Are you actually intending to splash around in the river?"

"Indeed we are. You should join us."

"My parents would be most displeased if I did."

"Who said they have to find out?"

He looked at me with uncertainty before giving in, "Tell no one," he said sternly, as he began to take off his shoes, waistcoat, and frock coat.

"Agreed."

After removing my shoes, I followed Giselle into the water and watched as she splashed around, getting her dress completely drenched in the process. "There goes another dress," I muttered. As Jonathan stepped into the river, I gathered up as much water as I could with my hands and splashed him. He stood there for a moment before a small grin emerged on his face. Before I knew it, we were all splashing each other like careless children. And by looking at Jonathan, I could hardly believe that he was a refined gentleman from a strict, noble family.

CHAPTER ELEVEN

As I laid in bed, staring up at the ceiling, the memories of the afternoon spun through my head like a wild tornado. I could scarcely believe that I had actually splashed around in the water like a child. I was ashamed of the way I had acted. I must have seemed very undignified to Miss Hoffman. Despite my own humiliation though, I had actually enjoyed every carefree minute of it.

Luckily, my family had not even noticed that my clothes were drenched and my hair was messed up. If my mother would have taken notice, surely she would have thought that I had tried to drown myself. She tended to think that I wanted to kill myself for some reason. I will admit that I have mentioned it a few times; however, I had never actually gone through with it.

"There is no use in lying here all night," I groaned, as I got out of bed, walked over to my desk, and poured myself a tall glass of water. As I gulped down the cool, refreshing liquid, my hand came to rest on my damp shirt, which hung over the back of the chair.

My previous conversation with Miss Hoffman then came to mind. I was still shocked by what she had told me. Her story would certainly explain her father's behaviour and their sudden arrival. It dawned on me that the Hoffmans would have never moved here if it had not been for those two unfortunate events. While that would mean that Matthew would have never had his heart broken, I was actually glad that they had come to England.

I was unsure of whether or not to consider her a friend, but I did trust her to a certain degree, and I had even enjoyed the time we spent walking in silence. By now, I could clearly see that Miss Hoffman would not have been happy with Matthew. Perhaps, deep down, I was even glad that she had rejected him.

Just then there came a knock at my door. "Jonathan, are you awake?" Vincent asked.

"Yes," I answered.

He opened the door and stepped into the room. "What are you doing up at this hour? It is nearly midnight."

"I could ask you the same question," I replied. "Why are you here?"

"I was just wondering where you disappeared to earlier at the Hoffmans'."

"I went for a walk and ended up near the town," I told him. That was partially true, for I did go for a walk, just in the opposite direction.

His jaw nearly dropped to the ground. "How on earth did you manage to walk all the way to town without dropping dead?"

"I have had plenty of practise," I replied, setting my empty glass back on the desk.

"Have you ever tried to run away?" he asked all of a sudden.

I was taken by surprise. "It has crossed my mind, but I knew that Mother would send the bloodhounds after me if I did. I did try once when I was thirteen, although Matthew found me and started rambling on about his life and then I ended up running away from him."

He smirked, "That sounds about right." He then placed his hand on the back of the chair to lean on it, but removed it immediately. "Why is your shirt wet?"

"I spilled water on it earlier."

He eyed the shirt with suspicion. "There are times that you completely baffle me, Jonathan. I can never figure out what is going on in your head."

"That is probably a good thing. If you did, you would most likely end up screaming like Mr. Hoffman."

"You thought that was weird too? It seemed like he was in agonizing pain, and yet all he did was bump his leg," he commented.

"Yes, it was quite peculiar," I agreed.

"I feel sorry for his daughter though," he stated. "She seems like a wonderful young lady."

"What is your impression of her?"

"I cannot recall ever speaking to her, but I imagine that she is lonely."

"Why do you say that?"

"The only person I have ever seen her talking to is Miss Abbott. We can all imagine how good a friend *she* must be," he explained. "I imagine that having only her as a friend must get tiresome; although, I could say the same thing about your friend."

"I imagine that Miss Abbott must be just as irritating as Matthew."

"I am afraid that nobody seems to know much about the Hoffmans. At times it feels like they are hiding something from everyone."

"I suppose that some secrets are better left undiscovered. It is most likely just some minor incident about which they are embarrassed."

"There is one thing that I do know about her. She is undoubtedly the most beautiful woman I have ever laid eyes on."

"I actually agree with you for once."

"Really? I could arrange an informal meeting with her if you want," he offered.

"Just because I find a woman beautiful, does not mean I want to meet her."

"I was just trying to help."

"Well, if you are done helping me now, you can go back to your own bedroom."

"Fine," he relented, taking his leave.

Feeling the need to clear my head after that, I put on a dry shirt and went out onto the balcony. From the balcony, I could catch a small glimpse of Portsmouth. Most of the town was fast asleep, yet I could still see a few lights on in the shops of the lower part of town.

I began to wonder what my life would be like had I been born to a family with less money. Would I be happy? Would my family actually understand me? Although I doubted that I would be able to do the work that some men my age could easily do, I often enjoyed thinking about things like that.

Then I gazed up at the stars in the sky. I would come out here and stargaze whenever I was unable to sleep. I enjoyed testing my knowledge of the constellations, such as Ursa Minor. I was well aware that some might find such a hobby extremely boring, but to me it was fascinating. In a way, you could say that gazing up at the stars helped me to feel closer to God.

Why had I been given a life that was filled with so much misery? There seemed to be nothing good about it at times; however, I trusted that God knew what he was doing and would hopefully improve my life. With a sudden yawn, I decided that I had best go back inside and try to get some sleep. If I stayed up all night again, I would surely be a walking corpse in the morning.

CHAPTER TWELVE

My life had been filled with pure misery for the past month. I now dreaded social events more than ever, due to the constant presence of Matthew Caldwell. Simply being in the same building with him made me uncomfortable. He would stare at me as if he were watching my every move. I felt like a lone deer being stalked by a predator.

Surprisingly enough, there had been many times that I had been able to speak with Jonathan Gilmore. Of course our conversations were quite brief and inconspicuous; however, by now I had come to regard him as someone that I could trust.

"Helene, do you think I could borrow that dark green dress of yours?" Louise asked, as I sat by my window and read a book. "Are you even listening to me?"

"It is hard not to listen to you, Louise," I teased. "Why would you want to borrow my dress? You have plenty of beautiful dresses of your own."

"That is very true, but James really likes the colour green and I do not have a decent green dress in my entire wardrobe!" she exclaimed.

I rolled my eyes and placed my book on the window sill. "All right, I was planning on wearing my purple dress to the ball next week anyway."

Just then, a man on horseback rode up in front of the house and began to dismount. Louise rushed over to get a better look. "Who is that?" she asked.

From where I was seated, I could see why she had rushed over to the window. The man was indeed very handsome with his warm, chocolate-coloured eyes and sun-kissed brown hair. His skin was beautifully tanned, from what I guessed to be the result of spending many hours outside, and his chiseled chin and jaw were lined with an attractive amount of stubble. "That must be Mr. Johnson," I said.

"Who?"

"The man who is going to be living with us for a while," I explained.

"Forget about James. I want Mr. Johnson!" she swooned.

"Louise, you have not even met him yet!" I protested.

"How do you know him?" she asked.

"He is a distant relative of Charlotte's who's in town for business reasons. He needed a place to stay and we were recommended."

"In that case, you can keep your green dress. I will be wearing my yellow one," she declared.

"Helene, come and greet our guest!" my mother called.

"What are you waiting for?" Louise asked, grabbing my wrist and rushing me out of the room and down the stairs.

"Mr. Johnson, this is our daughter, Helene, and her good friend Louise Abbott," my father introduced us. "Girls, this is Mr. William Johnson. He will be staying with us for a while."

I yanked my wrist from Louise's grasp, "It is a pleasure to meet you, sir."

"The pleasure is mine," he replied, smiling at me. "Charlotte has told me much about you."

"Is that so?" I asked.

"All good I hope," Louise interrupted.

"Of course," he replied.

"Helene, would you show our guest to his room?" Mother requested. "The council will be arriving soon."

"All right," I agreed. "Right this way." He followed me upstairs, down the short corridor, and into the guest room where he put his suitcase on the bed.

"You must thank your parents for allowing me to stay here."

"It is no problem; however, you must bear in mind that this room is normally inhabited by Charlotte's four-year-old daughter. You may find a few stray dolls lying around."

"That is quite all right. I have slept in far worse bedrooms."

I could not help but smile when he looked at me. "Might I ask where you are from, Mr. Johnson?"

"I reside in Southampton," he replied. "Might I ask what your mother was referring to earlier when she spoke of a council arriving?"

"My father is on the church council as the graveyard manager. There are a couple of families arriving to discuss the renovations being made. It is unfortunate that it had to be today; however, the reverend insisted," I explained.

He nodded in understanding. "Is that why Charlotte referred to your father as the Grim Reaper?"

I tried to restrain myself from laughing. "Charlotte calls him that because he is often quite grumpy. The fact that he manages the graveyard only adds to her list of reasons."

"As long as I do not have to worry about him trying to kill me in my sleep, I should be fine," he joked.

"He is not that bad. We just like to tease each other," I assured him.

"I am glad to meet a family that still cares for one another. There are not many left in this part of the world."

"That is very true."

"Helene!" Father called. *"Der Rat ist hier!"*

"The rat is here?" he questioned. "What rat?"

I rushed to the window to see who had arrived. To my dismay, I saw both Matthew and James in the midst of the group. My heart skipped a beat. "You must excuse me, but the council is here," I excused myself, trudging out of the room. With every step I took, my dread grew and grew. Then, when I reached the staircase, everyone looked up at me.

"Miss Hoffman, it is nice to see you again," Mr. Caldwell greeted, as I came down the stairs.

"It is nice to see you as well," I replied as politely as I could. Out of the corner of my eye, I could see that Matthew was once again staring at me. I tried to avoid his gaze as our parents started to discuss the renovations, but then my eyes met Jonathan's. His very expression told me that Matthew had come against his will. I nodded my head slightly to show him that I understood. Then everyone fell silent and turned their attention towards Mr. Johnson, who was standing at the top of the staircase.

"Allow me to introduce our guest," father said. "This is Mr. William Johnson. He will be staying with us for some time."

As he slowly came down the stairs, I could see that he was shocked about something. He seemed to be looking at the Gilmores in particular. It was almost as if he recognized them.

"It is nice to meet you, young man," Mr. Gilmore said, extending his hand.

Mr. Johnson did not say a word; however, I could tell that he was scared as he refused Mr. Gilmore's handshake. Things became awkward after that. Thankfully, my father managed to break the silence. "Shall we head into the parlour?" he asked.

"I think that is a good idea," Mr. Caldwell agreed, as everyone swarmed into the room.

"Might I have the pleasure of your company on a walk, Miss Hoffman?" Mr. Johnson asked.

Desperate to escape another afternoon spent with Matthew, I eagerly accepted. "Of course."

He grabbed his hat and opened the door for me before following me outside. We strolled through the apple orchard in the backyard for quite some time. He seemed to be just as relieved as I was to be out of the house, for some odd reason.

"I was not aware that you knew the Governor and his family," he said.

"They were the first people we met when we arrived in England. Although, we are not exactly friends, we do tend to spend quite a bit of time at the Gilmore manor," I explained. "Do you know them?"

"I met them briefly when I used to live here."

"I was not aware that you used to live here in Portsmouth."

He nodded. "That was five years ago, so I doubt that they would remember me."

"You do not seem to be very fond of them," I observed.

"I do not know them very well, but I have heard that they are not the most friendly."

"I used to see them the same way you do, but then I came to understand them a bit better," I told him. "Mrs. Gilmore has such high expectations. She expects her children to marry the people she selects for them without any complaints."

"How do you know this?" he asked.

"Miss Caroline Gilmore happens to be my music teacher."

He quickly changed the topic. "If my eyes were not mistaken, I would say that there is someone in your house that you dislike as well."

I sighed. "I am afraid that it is the reverend's sons who make me uneasy. I cannot say that I dislike them; however, they do seem to dislike me."

"I find it hard to believe that anyone could dislike such a beautiful woman as yourself," he complimented me, handing me an apple.

"You are mistaken. I am not nearly as beautiful as Miss Gilmore or Miss Abbott," I claimed, taking the apple and biting into it.

"You underestimate yourself. I think that you are just as beautiful as Miss Gilmore. You should stop comparing yourself to others."

"Not everyone thinks the same way you do."

"I suppose that you are correct," he said with a grin. "Thank you for accompanying me, but I should go inside and unpack now."

"I will let you know when our guests are gone," I replied as I watched him leave.

As soon as he was out of sight, Louise ran up to me from behind the house. "Helene, if you do not snatch him, I will," she declared.

"What are you talking about?" I asked.

"You are so naive! It is obvious that he likes you!" she exclaimed.

"Perhaps as a person, but I certainly do not believe that he likes me in the way that you are referring to."

"He was flirting with you for goodness sake!"

"I take it that you were eavesdropping on us the whole time." I rolled my eyes. "I do not believe that he was flirting with me either. Besides, I have barely known him for half an hour."

"Who cares about that? He is almost as handsome as Jonathan Gilmore! Surely even you cannot deny that."

"I will admit that he is; however, you know very well that my opinions are not based on appearances."

"Fine, if you do not want him then you can help me catch him," she said happily, as she skipped off.

"Poor Mr. Johnson," I mumbled to myself, as I followed after her.

CHAPTER THIRTEEN

The Seymour family's estate was quite similar in size to my family's, although it did not have as much land as ours. Despite this, the manor was still impressive. My family had been friends with the Seymour family for as long as I could remember. While I did not know their only son, Edward, very well, he was rumoured to be a clumsy dancer. However, that did not bother me.

What did bother me was the thought of my friend's arrival. I just knew that he would make a bee line straight towards me, and begin complaining about Miss Hoffman again. Over the course of the past month, he had done nothing but complain about her every action. Surely seeing her with the mysterious Mr. Johnson would only add to his complaints.

"You look happy," Vincent noted, as he came to stand in front of me.

"I am dreading the moment that Matthew walks through the door," I replied.

"I thought you enjoyed his company," he commented.

"There are times that he can be quite tolerable; however, there are also times when I feel like strangling him," I explained. "If he has something to complain about, you cannot get him to be quiet."

"He sounds a bit like our mother," he joked.

At that remark, I managed a small grin. "You may have a point there."

"At least I managed to cheer you up a bit," he said with a smile.

Just then, the Caldwells made their entrance, and as expected, Matthew came straight towards me. "I would not get too used to it," I told Vincent.

"Try to resist the urge to strangle him," my brother said, patting me on the shoulder before vanishing into the crowd.

"Can you believe how Miss Hoffman is acting?" Matthew fumed.

"What is it now?" I asked.

"Flinging herself at a man she has only known for a few days. She is clearly trying to make me miserable."

I gave a frustrated sigh. "You were staring at her. She probably just wanted to get away from you."

"Perhaps he would be a good match for her. They are both undoubtedly rude. Did you not see how he refused your father's handshake?"

"I certainly did; however, I also saw the look on his face. He looked like a scared dog."

"Lots of people are afraid of your father. It seems to run in the family."

"Why does everyone enjoy insulting me?" I asked, sounding slightly offended.

"Sorry," he apologized. "If it is any consolation, the women do not seem to be afraid of you."

I rolled my eyes. "I wish that they were."

"There he is," he grumbled, glancing at Mr. Johnson as he came in with the Hoffmans. "He must think that he is so much better than me."

"Would you quit complaining and be quiet for once? We know nothing about him."

"Fine," he grumbled. "Perhaps I should go over there and interrogate him."

"Why do you care if she has feelings for him?"

He relented. "I cannot seem to get over her, even though she broke my heart and humiliated me."

"You really are an ignorant fool," I muttered.

"What?"

"You are making yourself miserable. If you continue to be like this, you will end up being humiliated again."

"I do not intend to profess my feelings to her again," he assured me. "Believe me when I say that I have learned my lesson."

"That is a relief."

"Why have you always been so against my feelings for her? Besides your disbelief in them, of course."

"You know nothing about her. You have no clue about her past, nor do you know anything of her character other than your recent opinion that she is rude. Everything that you know about her is an assumption."

"I have tried to remedy that in every way I know how. She is as much a puzzle to me as you are to your brother," he retorted. "The only thing that I know for certain is that she is not interested in me."

"Try reminding yourself of that before you act next time. Now, if you will excuse me, I would prefer to spend the rest of the evening without hearing another complaint." With that, I walked away and headed into the corridor, where I hid in the hopes of being alone.

"Are you hiding from your brother or your friend?" a familiar voice asked.

I turned my head to find Miss Hoffman standing at the other end of the corridor. "Both," I informed her. Even though I had wanted to be alone, for some strange reason, I did not seem to mind if she was in my company. "Are you enjoying the ball?"

She shook her head and came to stand beside me. "I am enjoying it as much as you, I fear."

"How is your guest enjoying it?" I asked.

She groaned. "He has not had the chance to enjoy himself. Louise has been following him the entire evening."

"Tell me that you are joking," I said with astonishment. "What does James think of this?"

"James is far too intoxicated to even notice."

"How can you tell?" I wondered. "He acts no differently than usual."

"I have seen my brother when he is intoxicated. You can usually tell by looking at the eyes."

I looked at her with surprise. "I might have to put that information to good use. I believe that my brother may have been intoxicated a couple of times."

"I would not doubt that," she said with a giggle. "With how many different women has he danced?"

"I have long lost count," I chuckled. "Sometimes, when I become bored at events like these, I attempt to count all of the women he dances with. I can never keep track of him though, so it normally does not work."

"When I was younger, I used to sneak a book along to the balls. Then, when my mother had turned her back, I would slip away and read in the music room at your family's estate."

"You managed to find your way from the ballroom to the upstairs music room without the help of an escort?"

She nodded. "Caroline gave me permission to do so if I ever wanted to get away from everyone."

"Perhaps I should try that the next time we host a ball."

We stayed there for quite a while in silence. Eventually, she broke the silence and asked me an odd question. "Did you know Mr. Johnson before last week?"

"I do not believe so. However it seemed like he knew my father," I replied. "Has he told you anything about himself?"

"The only thing that he has told me is that he used to live here in Portsmouth five years ago."

"My father knows nearly every citizen of this town, and he has never known of a man by that name. Perhaps he is lying?"

"I am uncertain of what to think of him. Something must have happened, because he was quite desperate to leave the house," she observed. "It seemed like he was looking at one person in particular, but I could not tell whether it was your mother or Caroline."

"Jonathan?" Vincent called all of a sudden. "Where are you?"

"I should go find Louise and ensure that she has not driven the poor Mr. Johnson insane," she said, and then hurried down the corridor and disappeared, just as Vincent peeked his head around the corner.

"What are you doing back here?" he asked.

"Well, I was trying to avoid hearing any further complaints, but it would seem that God has different plans."

"Never mind that," he rolled his eyes. "The most bizarre thing just happened. I went to introduce myself to Mr. Johnson, but he rushed off before I had even told him who I was."

"Did he seem afraid of something?"

"Yes, he started looking around as if someone were watching him," he replied.

"I have absolutely no idea what is wrong with him. I have my suspicions that it has something to do with our mother," I stated.

There certainly was something peculiar about this man's behaviour. It was as if he were trying to hide something from us all. Perhaps something had happened that none of us knew about. I suppose that if he had lived in the lower part of town, then Father would not have known him. I shook it out of my mind. It was none of my business and I had no reason to think about it any further.

CHAPTER FOURTEEN

I found myself lost in thought
as we rode through the forest on our way to the Gilmore estate.
Questions swirled around in my head. I could not comprehend why
Mr. Johnson had been acting so strangely, and to make things even
more bizarre, none of the Gilmores seemed to know him.

He had seemed quite charming to me. However, I wondered if
it had just been an act. From what I had overheard the other night,
it appeared that he was afraid of one person in particular, and I too
had a feeling that it was Mrs. Gilmore. Perhaps he had accidentally
offended her in some way and she was angry. It seemed to make the
most sense after all.

As the carriage came to a stop in front of the manor, I thought
of asking Caroline if she knew anything. She was the only person I
could think of asking without asking Mrs. Gilmore directly. Even
if I could ask her, she would probably just tell me to mind my
own business.

I stepped out of the carriage and followed my parents inside.
Once again, the butler arrived and escorted us upstairs, but this time
I took off towards the music room before he could even tell me
where to find her. I was determined to find out why Mr. Johnson
was behaving so strangely.

I walked up to the door and knocked gently. "Come in," called Caroline. I opened the door to find her seated at the piano, ready to begin the lesson.

"Forgive me for being late," I apologized. "My father lost his cane and we had to turn the house upside down to find it."

"That is quite all right. I have not been waiting too long," she replied with a giggle.

I smiled and took a seat beside her. She began to teach me how to play the Bach Prelude and before I knew it, I could play it alongside her with only a few mistakes. Halfway through the lesson, we decided to take a break and have some tea.

"Might I ask you something?" I requested.

"Of course," she replied, taking a sip of her tea.

"Do you know Mr. Johnson?"

Her eyes widened. "Why do you ask that?"

"I have noticed that he seems to be afraid of your family," I explained. "I was just wondering if you knew anything about him."

She placed her cup of tea on the end table and got up from her seat. She walked over to the window and looked out at the town. "I did know him five years ago," she said.

"Did something happen between him and your parents?"

"There was an incident. Although it was not between him and my parents," she began to explain. "We were in love with each other, or at least that was what I had thought."

It was my turn to be surprised. "You loved him?" I asked.

She nodded. "I loved him more than anyone I have ever known on this earth; however, he did not feel the same way about me."

"What happened?"

"The day before his departure, he was caught with another woman from town," she said, beginning to cry. "I was told that he had left to elope with her."

I sat there in a state of utter shock. I could not believe that Mr. Johnson had betrayed Caroline like that. It might have explained his behaviour if he had been guilty, but I was convinced that it was fear instead of guilt that caused his bizarre reaction. "Where did you learn this? Who told you?" I asked.

She dried her eyes on her handkerchief. "It was my mother who discovered it. She was the only one who knew of us."

When I heard her say that, a piece of the puzzle clicked into place. It was just as I had predicted. Mrs. Gilmore was very much involved in this. "That explains so much," I said to myself.

"Promise me that you will not tell anyone about this, Helene," she pleaded. "He may have broken my heart, but I do not want to disgrace him."

I understood why she would not want people to know. To tell the world what happened would disgrace her as well as Mr. Johnson, and I was certain that the Gilmores did not want to be socially disgraced. "I would never try to disgrace anyone," I assured her. "However, I do want to hear what Mr. Johnson has to say about this."

"Helene, if you are planning on making him feel guilty, I must ask that you reconsider."

"If what you have told me is true, he should have enough guilt already. I simply want to know his side of the story before I judge him."

She turned to face me, "You want to learn his side of the story?"

I nodded, "I do not believe that your mother has told you the true story; however, I will not know for certain until I speak with him."

"If you could discover the truth for me, I would be in your debt."

With a smile, I rose to my feet. "I will try my hardest for your sake."

"Well, I suppose that our time is gone," she said, glancing at the clock. "I will see you next week."

With a nod, I took my leave. While strolling down the lavish corridor, I began to stare out the windows as I passed them by. The strange behaviour of Mr. Johnson now made more sense. He had been shocked to see Caroline again, but at the same time he was afraid of Mrs. Gilmore. If he was guilty, he would have been afraid of being exposed. If he was innocent, then he would have been afraid of something that Caroline did not know about.

As I approached the entrance hall, I saw no sign of my mother or father anywhere. I groaned with frustration. It would seem that they had yet not finished their tea. "Why must tea time take so long?" I asked myself, as I began to examine the ceiling designs.

"Miss Hoffman, what are you doing down here?" a very familiar voice asked.

I gazed up towards the staircase and there stood Jonathan Gilmore at the very top. Even from a distance, you could see how handsome he was. *"He truly is the most handsome man in town,"* I thought briefly, before shaking it out of my head. Why did I care whether he was handsome or not? "I am waiting for my parents to finish their tea," I explained.

"Well then, perhaps you would want to accompany me on a walk?" he offered.

"Only if you do not mind my company."

"Not at all," he replied, opening the front door for me. "I have come to enjoy being in your company."

"I do not see why anyone would enjoy being near me," I joked, making my way out into the garden. "Louise says that I am as dull as a doorknob."

He chuckled lightly as he walked beside me. "I enjoy being around dull doorknobs much more than my irritating brother."

"I can assume that he complains a lot, and that the topic of his complaints is your refusal to dance."

"You are very observant."

I grinned, "You may be correct; however, I fear that my observations sometimes make me jump to conclusions."

"Not to mention that you are quite wise."

"I prefer the term 'practical', although my friend prefers the term 'boring'."

"Tell me something," he said, stopping all of a sudden. "Why do you tolerate Miss Abbott the way you do?"

"Why do you tolerate Matthew Caldwell?"

He pondered my question for a moment. "I suppose you could say that he is my only friend."

"Louise is the closest thing that I have ever had to a friend. I am afraid to say that I spent my childhood playing with my brothers," I explained. "What about you? Did you ever play with your siblings as a child?"

"We did at one point, but we ended up breaking a vase and Mother never let us play together again after that."

"The more I hear of your mother, the more I come to think of her as a jailer."

"You must be very brave to say that," he noted. "Most people are afraid to even mention her."

"That is nothing; Charlotte calls my father the Grim Reaper."

He struggled to keep himself from laughing. "I would say that it suits him."

"People are often intimidated by him; however, I could not ask for a better father."

"Why is that?"

"You would have to see him in his private life to realize this, but he is actually a caring and thoughtful individual. He has experienced a lot of pain in his life, but then again, who has not?"

"I always imagined him as a type of Ebenezer Scrooge from *A Christmas Carol.*"

"He could be Mr. Scrooge, if Mr. Scrooge happened to speak German," I replied with a giggle.

He smiled at me slightly. "How well do you know German?"

"Ich weiß es ganz gut," I replied in German.

He was taken back by this. "I did not quite get that."

"I know it quite well. It was the first language I ever knew."

He stared at me with his dreamy grey eyes, as if I had just said something that fascinated him. Then his gaze became distracted by something behind me. "How would I tell you that your parents are looking for you in German?"

I glanced at them briefly before looking back at Jonathan. "I should get going."

"And I should return to the library in case someone finds me missing and thinks that I have been abducted," he joked.

I could not help but laugh. "Good day, Mr. Gilmore," I said, making my way back to the carriage. When I looked back a minute later, he was nowhere to be found.

CHAPTER FIFTEEN

There was tension in the air as Vincent, our father, and I galloped off into the forest. Father had suggested that we go out for a hunting trip. Personally I had not been fond of the idea. Normally, I would not mind it if he wanted to spend time with us; however, all of the previous hunting trips had ended in one of us getting fed up and returning home early.

We had taken a small pack of approximately ten hunting dogs and one servant along to assist us. The dogs were to help us gather the foxes and the servant was to ensure that we did not start strangling each other; although, he always seemed to stay out of our arguments. "Remind me why I agreed to come on another hunting trip with you two," I grumbled as we came to a stop.

"I believe you agreed to come so that Father would stop pestering you," Vincent explained.

"Why are you so against it, Jonathan?" Father asked.

"I do not enjoy hunting as much as you do," I stated.

"Well, what would you like to do?" he asked as he prepared his gun.

"A casual ride or walk through the forest would be sufficient."

"You do enough walking as it is."

"I just do not see why we always have to go hunting."

"The hunting trip is a tradition in our family. My father used to take me hunting three times a year."

Our grandfather, after whom Vincent had been named, had not been a favourite of ours. He had died when I was only four years old, but I could still remember him quite well. He had been very strict and would not tolerate any unruliness. Perhaps that was why Father had ended up the way he did.

"You are not your father and we are not you," I replied. "Thank goodness for that."

"What is wrong with me?"

"Nothing, you just tend to ignore us."

"Here we go," Vincent mumbled.

"I will have you know that I take more notice than you realize," he protested.

"When is my birthday?" I tested him.

He aimed his gun, this way and that. "You were born on February the third."

"That is Caroline's birthday."

"Well, then it must be August the thirty-first."

I shook my head. "That is Vincent's birthday. I was born on June the tenth."

He glanced at me with confusion, "Are you certain?"

I nodded. "I cannot believe that you do not even remember the day your own son was born."

"Will you two stop it?" Vincent interrupted.

"Can we discuss this later?" Father asked, firing his gun suddenly.

As soon as the gun was fired, my attention was drawn to Vincent who was found clutching his arm in agonizing pain. He let out a horrifying scream that could only be compared to that of Mr. Hoffman. My eyes widened with shock as I watched him fall from his horse and hit the ground with a thud.

"Vincent!" I yelled, as I dismounted and raced to his side. I examined his body, praying that he had not been fatally wounded.

I ripped off his coat to find blood gushing down his arm. "Go fetch the doctor and tell him to come to the manor immediately!" I told the servant.

"Of course, sir!" He nodded and rode off.

"He is losing a lot of blood and is unconscious. We need to get him back to the estate," I explained as I slung his good arm around my neck and set him up on his horse. I mounted my horse quickly and rushed back towards the estate, holding the reigns of my brother's horse and guiding it as I held him in the saddle.

We rode as fast as we could. I thanked God that we had not gone too far from home. My only hope was that Vincent would not share the same fate as Mr. Hoffman. It sent shivers down my spine, just imagining him with only one arm. As soon as we arrived, Caroline and the butler rushed out. "What happened?" Caroline asked as I helped Vincent down.

"We will fill you in later. For now we need to get him to his bedroom," I replied, as I slung his arm over my shoulder and hurried him into the house.

"Are we to drag him all the way upstairs, sir?" the butler asked.

"It is the only way," I told him. "Someone grab his legs and we will try to hoist him up the staircase." Father and the butler grabbed his legs while I grabbed hold of him under his arms and we began our slow journey up the stairs.

When we finally reached the top, we let him flop to the floor for a moment. Then we helped him back up and dragged him into his bedroom. We laid him down onto the bed where we began to tear off his waistcoat and shirt to see how bad the wound was. Caroline gasped with shock when the wound was uncovered. "Do you want me to get Mother?" she asked.

"I am in no mood to tolerate her right now; however, you can go keep an eye out for the doctor. We sent a servant to fetch him."

"All right," she said, rushing out of the room.

Father whispered a prayer, "God, please make him be all right."

"Everything depends on how quickly the doctor can get here," I told him. "If the wound is left untended for too long he will lose his arm completely."

He looked at me with confusion, "Where did you learn this?"

"When you spend as much time in the library as I do, you are bound to learn things."

"You always were fond of books. As an infant, the only way I could get you to stop crying was to read to you."

"You used to read to me?" I asked with surprise.

He nodded. "You were too young to remember."

I began to feel guilty for how I had acted. "I am sorry for what I said earlier. I should have kept my mouth shut."

He shook his head. "It is I who should apologize. I must admit that I do not pay as much attention as I should. If you want to do something different next time, let me know."

Before I could reply, Caroline burst into the room with Dr. Weston. "The doctor is here!" she exclaimed.

Dr. Weston immediately went to work. He began to examine the wound, wiping away some blood in the process. "What exactly happened to him?" he asked.

"He was accidentally shot," I informed him.

"I see," he said, looking me up and down. "Did you drag him all the way from the forest?"

I nodded my head. "Why do you ask?"

"Well, it would explain why you are covered in blood," he pointed out.

I glanced down at myself and found that he was quite correct. My coat was dripping with blood. "Good Lord! It looks like *I* was shot!" I exclaimed.

"Will he be all right?" Father asked.

"If I can remove the bullet and clean the wound, his arm should be fine. Although, it will take many months to heal," he assured us.

We were relieved to hear that. Dr. Weston was a fine doctor and I was certain that, with God's help, he would have the knowledge that he needed in order to treat Vincent's arm. Suddenly, I realized just how fragile life was, and how quickly people could be taken. I quickly shoved that thought into the back of my mind and headed down the hall towards my room, to change into some clean clothes before Mother saw me and thought that I had attempted to take my own life.

CHAPTER SIXTEEN

The household was in a state of disarray as my family got ready for church. Alexander was chasing after Giselle, Charlotte was struggling to calm Henry down, and Father was hobbling around, looking for his cane as usual. All the while, I sat at the bottom of the stairs and watched. I always enjoyed Sundays for the performance my family gave.

My mind then wandered to the issue of Caroline and Mr. Johnson. I had not had a chance to confront him since Caroline had told me her side of the story. Unfortunately, he had been gone on business a lot lately. At the moment, he happened to be outside enjoying the fresh morning air. *"This might be the only opportunity I have to confront him,"* I thought.

I got up from my seat on the stairs and went out to find him. I found him out on the back porch, sitting on a bench and reading a book that appeared to be the Bible. "What passage are you reading?" I asked.

"Verses four to eight in the thirteenth chapter of first Corinthians," he replied, looking up at me. "Did you need something?"

"I was wondering if I could ask you something."

"Of course," he said, setting his Bible down beside him. "What do you want to know?"

"Why did you leave five years ago?"

He seemed to sadden slightly. "It is complicated."

"Does it have something to do with Caroline?"

He was surprised. "What?"

"Caroline told me her side of the story a few days ago. Now I want to know whether it is true or not."

"What did she tell you?" he asked

"She told me that you left her to elope with some other woman."

"Where did she hear that?" he asked, his eyes wide with shock.

"That was what her mother told her," I informed him.

"That is not true!" he exclaimed.

"Please tell me what happened then."

He was silent for a moment. "The day before I left, Mrs. Gilmore came to my uncle's shop and threatened to run him out of business if I did not leave town," he explained.

"That explains so much," I stated.

"You actually believe me?" he questioned with amazement.

"Of course I do," I assured him. "I can tell that it is not guilt that drove you to act rather strangely in front of the Gilmores. Besides, everyone in town knows that Mrs. Gilmore is not the most pleasant woman alive. Nonetheless, you should talk to Caroline and tell her what really happened."

He sighed. "Even if she did believe me, how would I manage to speak with her without her mother catching me?"

"Getting her to believe you will not be a problem," I assured him. I thought about it for a while before an idea came to mind. "Are you coming with us to church?"

"I was planning on it," he replied. "Why do you ask?"

"If I can get her to follow me behind the church, you should be able to talk to her for a few minutes before the service starts."

"Would you really do that for me?"

I nodded. "Caroline is unsure of who she should believe, but I believe that she still cares for you."

He smiled sincerely. "If I can talk to her for even a minute, I will be in your debt."

"Think nothing of it."

"Helene, you can tell Mr. Johnson that we are ready to go!" Mother called from inside.

"All right!" I called back.

We walked all the way around the house and joined everyone, except Charlotte, in the carriage. Mother and Charlotte would take turns staying at home with the children while the rest of us went to church. It was strange not having them around. I happened to miss them very much. They certainly made life more interesting for me.

"You have not told us much about yourself, Mr. Johnson," Alexander commented. "What do you do for a living?"

"I work for a farmer in Southampton. He provides me with a bed for the night and food to eat in exchange for my labour."

"I can assume that you are out here doing business for your employer, then?"

"That is correct," he replied. "Although, I also came to visit my uncle."

"How long are you planning on staying with us?" Mother asked.

"I intend to be gone before the end of next week."

"You are leaving so soon?" I asked.

"I fear that I am a far greater burden to the people around me then I realize."

"I would hardly call it a burden. It is no different from when Alexander was living with us," Mother assured him.

"Are you implying that you would like me to move back in?" Alexander asked.

"It would make no difference. You are always at the house, anyway," Father teased.

We soon arrived at church, where Alexander and Mr. Johnson stepped out and began to help the rest of us down. It was nothing more than a small country church with a large graveyard to the left side of it. The congregation normally consisted of seventy to eighty people, and although the number of people was small in comparison to some, the church was usually filled to maximum capacity.

I searched the crowd for Caroline, and after a few moments, I found her arguing with Louise. "I cannot stretch your lessons an hour longer than everyone else's," Caroline informed her. "It would be unfair to the other girls."

"Helene, convince her to extend my lesson by an hour!" Louise pleaded.

"You would be stealing time away from *my* lessons. Why would I help you with that?" I defended myself.

"Hmph! Some friend you are!" she declared as she walked off.

"Should you not be going after her?" Caroline asked.

"She will forget about it soon enough," I assured her. "May I speak with you somewhere more private?"

"I suppose," she replied.

I led her behind the church just as I had planned and got straight to the point. "I talked to Mr. Johnson."

"What did he say?" she asked.

"He told me that he left because your mother threatened to run his uncle out of business."

"Why would she do such a thing?"

"Perhaps he should explain it to you."

"What?" her eyes widened.

"She is telling you the truth, Caroline," Mr. Johnson joined in, coming up beside me.

Tears trickled down her face at the very sight of him. "Did you really leave to elope with another woman?" she asked.

"I must admit that your mother did see me with another woman. However, she was my cousin," he explained. "I would never wish to hurt you like that."

She buried her face in her hands. "I cannot believe that she lied to me," she sobbed.

He went and wrapped his arms around her in a comforting embrace. "It is all right," he hushed her.

At that moment, I decided to go find my family. While I walked, I found myself wondering if love actually did exist. Mr. Johnson seemed to genuinely care about Caroline, yet it seemed like there was something more behind it. I could not comprehend what it was. I quickly shook that notion out of my head. How could such a thing truly exist in a world where mothers forced their children into arranged marriages that only made them miserable?

While I was lost deep in thought, I bumped into someone unexpected. I looked up to find Vincent Gilmore staring back at me. "I am so sorry! I was not looking where I was going!" I apologized.

"You need not fear, Miss Hoffman. I was not exactly paying attention myself," he said with a charming smile.

That was when I happened to notice his arm, which was completely bandaged up. "Might I ask what happened to your arm?"

He looked slightly uncomfortable at the mention of his arm. "I had a bit of a hunting accident."

"You were shot?"

"I take it that you know what a hunting accident is," he replied with surprise.

"Unfortunately I do," I nodded. "Will your arm be all right?"

"Well, it hurts a lot when I move it, but it should heal with time."

"You are very fortunate to have survived. I hope that your family realizes that."

"My mother certainly does. She does not let me do anything for myself anymore."

I giggled, "You should enjoy it while it lasts."

"I will certainly take your advice."

Just then, Caroline came towards me. "Helene, may I speak with you?" she requested.

"Of course," I replied. "You must excuse me, Mr. Gilmore." He nodded and took his leave.

"I must thank you for what you did for me and William." She had a big smile on her face.

"I am pleased to have helped you," I replied.

"Is there any way that I can repay you?"

"Do not worry about it," I assured her.

She thought for a minute. "Perhaps you would like to come to London with my family?"

"London?" I repeated. My eyes widened with surprise. "Of course I would like to go. Although, I fear that I would only be a burden to your parents."

"You would not be a burden at all. My father gave me permission to bring one of my best students along."

"I am not, by far, the best of your students," I denied. "Are you sure that this is the way you wish to repay me? A simple 'thank you' is enough."

"I insist that you come with us."

I gave up. "If it means that much to you, I suppose that I could ask my father."

"We will be gone for a month; however, it should be all right with him if I can get my father to convince him."

"A whole month! What are you planning on doing in London for a month?"

"My aunt and uncle have an estate there. We have not visited them in many years. Jonathan was only five years old at the time of our last visit."

"I imagine that they will be very surprised to see him then," I giggled.

She giggled as well. "My aunt always used to mistake Vincent for Jonathan. If you do come along, you may have an opportunity to see my brothers get embarrassed."

"I will look forward to seeing that."

"Helene!" Father called.

"We are leaving next week Thursday, so you have a few days to convince him," she informed me before letting me go.

"I will try for your sake," I called, as I rushed to catch up with my family.

CHAPTER SEVENTEEN

I was so nervous as we rode through the streets of London. It felt like my stomach was twisted into a tight knot. The thing I was the most nervous about was meeting the Gilmores' relatives. Surely they would be even more sophisticated and snobby than Mrs. Gilmore. The thought of living with three snobs for a month made me question why I had even come.

By now you must be wondering how I ever managed to convince my father to let me go. I assure you that it was not easy. He had been against the idea in the beginning, but after he stopped to think about it, he began to realize that Mr. Gilmore would not let anything bad happen to me. On Thursday morning, I said my goodbyes to everyone and promised to bring back some gifts for Giselle and Henry.

Mr. Johnson had left two days before me. He told me that he could not be with Caroline, but that he would try to come back and visit again. Louise was devastated when I told her that he was a lowly farmer. Luckily, James had not even noticed her attempts to get Mr. Johnson's attention. Everything had turned out all right I suppose.

I glanced at the other passengers in the carriage. Caroline was seated on my left, with Mr. Gilmore directly opposite to me and Jonathan at his side. Vincent would have liked to ride with us; however, Mrs. Gilmore had insisted that he ride with her and a couple of servants. I thanked God that I did not have to be in the same carriage with her.

"What do you think of London so far, Miss Hoffman?" Mr. Gilmore asked.

"It is certainly bigger than I imagined," I commented.

"I suppose that it would seem large to someone who has never been here before," he replied.

"Is there anything in particular that you would like to see?" Caroline asked.

"I do not want to be a burden to any of you. Just being in London is enough."

"You are not a burden, Miss Hoffman," Mr. Gilmore assured me. "We are very pleased to have you with us."

"If I have time, I will try to show you around a bit. Although I fear that my aunt will keep me busy," Caroline stated.

We then came to a sudden stop. "Here we are," Mr. Gilmore announced as he got out and began to help Caroline and me down.

I was in awe of the four-storey building before my eyes. "It looks like a palace," I mumbled.

Jonathan, who was now standing on my left-hand side, must have heard me. "Our uncle is a Viscount," he whispered to me.

"That would explain it," I whispered back, as we were escorted inside by the butler.

"My masters will be down directly," he told us.

We waited for about five minutes before a woman appeared. "Charles, how are you my dear brother?" she greeted Mr. Gilmore.

"Josephine, it is good to see you again," he replied. "Where is your family?"

"Thomas is a bit preoccupied at the moment, but the others should be here soon," she explained, before turning her attention towards Vincent. "Jonathan, what has happened to your arm?"

Caroline and I tried to hold back our giggles. "You were right," I whispered.

"I am not Jonathan, Aunt Josephine," Vincent corrected her.

"Sorry, Vincent," she apologized. Just then, a man appeared with a very pretty young lady. "You remember my husband, Benjamin,"

"Of course I do," Mr. Gilmore replied, shaking the man's hand.

"I do not believe that we have met your guest," the woman noted, looking at me.

"This is Miss Helene Hoffman. She is one of Caroline's students."

"It is nice to meet you, Miss Hoffman," she introduced herself, smiling at me. "I am Josephine Edwards."

I managed to smile a bit. "It is nice to meet you, ma'am."

She motioned for her daughter to come forward, "This is my daughter, Anne,"

"It will be nice to have someone my own age around for a change," Anne said with a smile. I relaxed a little bit. Perhaps I had once again been too quick with my judgement. Mrs. Edwards and her family seemed quite friendly. Maybe they were the happier side of the family.

"I am sure that everyone is tired from their long journey, so I will have the servants escort you to your rooms," Mr. Edwards explained. "Anne, would you like to escort Miss Hoffman to her room personally?"

"Of course, Father," she replied, escorting me up two flights of stairs and down a long corridor. If I had thought that the corridors in the Gilmore manor were long, these were twice as long. I started to wonder how I would ever navigate through this palace for an entire month; however I was soon introduced to the man who would help me with that. "This is Mr. Brown. If you ever wish to explore the estate, I would advise that you ask him to escort you," she explained.

He reminded me a little bit of my father. He was an elderly man who wore glasses and did not seem to be very happy. In an attempt to lighten his mood, I smiled at him. "It is very nice to meet you, Mr. Brown," I greeted him.

"Now, let me show you your room," she said, as she showed me into a huge bedroom. It was unlike anything I had ever seen. My bedroom actually consisted of two rooms. One of them was called a sitting room, and according to Miss Edwards, it was appropriate for me to accept visitors in that room.

"I should introduce you to the servants who will be taking care of you," she said, as she began to introduce me to five more servants who would be at my disposal.

"All of these servants are at my disposal?" I asked, slowly becoming overwhelmed by the new life that I would be living.

"Are you not used to having this many servants under your command?" she asked.

"No."

"I can dismiss a few then. If Hannah and Edith could stay as Miss Hoffman's lady's maids then that would be fine." Three servants then left the room, leaving two women, one older and one younger. "Will three servants be enough?" I nodded my head in silence. "I shall take my leave now." Then she did just that.

I began to look around my new rooms with the curiosity of a child. The bed was so large that I could probably fit my entire family into it, including my five uncles back in Germany. Originally there had been six, but one of them had died of smallpox.

"Would you care for a nice, relaxing hot bath, miss? It may help you to unwind from your journey," the younger servant, Hannah suggested.

I looked at myself in the mirror and suddenly felt ashamed of my appearance. I was in London now after all. People would surely mock my appearance if I went around like this. "Perhaps a bath and a change of clothes would be best," I said.

"As you wish," the two lady's maids replied as they pushed Mr. Brown out of the room and commenced to bring out a tub of water.

CHAPTER EIGHTEEN

1 was back in Portsmouth, in the estate's ballroom, and once again dancing with Miss Hoffman. The only differences were that people were not staring at us and we were not arguing. People did not even seem to realize we were there. We all just circled round and round the room. I could not fathom why I was dancing, but from the expression on my face, I did not seem to mind at all. For some reason, I seemed to be enjoying myself for a change.

Then, just as the dance ended, I opened my eyes and I was back in London once again. I was quite disturbed by this dream. It made no sense to me. "Why on earth did I dream of that?" I mumbled, still half asleep.

"How should I know?" Vincent replied.

I looked to my right to find my brother sitting on the bed, staring at me. "What on earth are you doing in my bedroom?"

"You overslept and missed breakfast. Which is quite odd for you, because you are normally awake before everyone else," he explained.

"I missed breakfast? How did that happen?" I wondered.

He shrugged and jammed a piece of toast into my mouth. "If it makes you feel any better, you were not the only one absent."

"What do you mean?" I asked, taking a bite out of the warm bread.

"Miss Hoffman was not at breakfast either," he notified me.

All of a sudden, I felt anxious to get up and go find her. I began to rush about getting dressed and tidying up my hair. Then I stopped myself. Why on earth was I rushing to go see her?

"Have you always been this fast when it comes to getting dressed?" he teased.

I rolled my eyes, slowing down my pace and heading for the door. "You are ever-so amusing, Vincent."

"Where are you going?"

"Where do you think I am going?"

"To the library."

With a tiny smirk, I walked out of the room and proceeded to make my way to the library downstairs. People like Vincent would have found it nearly impossible to walk all the way across the estate, but I happened to have a fair amount of experience in walking.

I still could not fathom why I had dreamed of Miss Hoffman. In addition to that, I had been thinking about her a lot lately. I just could not seem to get her off my mind no matter what I did. It was as if my mind was trying to tell me something, but I could not process what it was.

Then I finally made it to the library. The Edwards' library was much larger than ours, but it happened to have fewer interesting books. Fortunately, they had all of William Shakespeare's works, whom incidentally was my favourite author, so I was quite satisfied with it.

Despite the fact that a lot of his works were so-called love stories, they were still entertaining to me. I had done quite a bit of research on him and knew that he had a younger brother named Edmund who followed him to London to become an actor. I enjoyed thinking that William and Edmund Shakespeare once lived in this very city.

Just then I heard someone enter the room. I quietly peered around the bookcase to see who it was. To my surprise, it was the very woman I had dreamed about: the one and only Miss Hoffman. She seemed to be amazed by the largeness of the library.

"It is large, is it not?" I asked, coming into view.

"It is the largest library I have ever seen!" she exclaimed.

"I heard that you missed breakfast," I commented.

She blushed slightly. "I accidentally slept in."

"You need not worry about it. I missed breakfast as well," I assured her.

"I find it hard to believe that you are the type of person to sleep in all of the time."

I chuckled, "You are quite correct. I suppose you could say that I got caught up in a dream."

"You must have been having a good dream," she said. I got lost in her smile for a moment. Vincent was right about her and I was big enough to admit it. She was the most beautiful woman I had ever seen.

"It was one of the better dreams that I have had actually," I claimed. "So, how are you liking London so far?"

"It has been a tad bit overwhelming; however, I am starting to adjust. I finally understand why noble families have so many servants."

"And why is that?" I wondered.

"To ensure that they do not get lost," she said with a giggle. "This is the largest house I have ever seen."

"It is quite large, even compared to my home."

"Speaking of homes, there is something I have been wondering. Your brother is to inherit your father's title and the estate, am I correct?"

"Indeed you are."

"What are you to inherit then?"

"I am to inherit a fair-sized fortune as well as an estate of my own near Southampton."

She seemed to sadden slightly for some reason. However, she quickly cheered up. "Really? That is where Mr. Johnson lives."

"Have you discovered why he is so afraid of my family?"

She hesitated, "I have indeed discovered the whole story, but I have promised to keep it a secret. I will tell you that it does very much involve your mother, though."

"When did you become so mysterious?" I asked.

"You are one to talk."

"I was not aware that I was considered mysterious."

"Obviously you have not heard what people say about you."

"Do I want to know what they say about me?"

"Most people do not know what to make of your character," I explained, "Some people think that you are arrogant and some think that you are just gloomy."

"What about you? What do you make of my character?"

She smirked slightly. "I see a man who understands me better than anyone else I have met. People may see you as arrogant, but in reality you are just misunderstood because of your dislike of social events."

I was surprised by her words. "I must admit that you understand me better than anyone else as well. No one else even cares to take the time to get to know me."

"I would not say that. Your elder brother seems to be trying."

"Vincent is just being annoying."

"I do not think that Vincent is trying to annoy you. Who else would tear himself away from his own enjoyment every single time there is a ball, just to speak with you, knowing that you will just shut him out again?"

Her words pierced into my heart. "I never thought of it that way."

"I know what it is like to have an elder brother that you find annoying at times, but he cannot understand you if you do not let him into your life."

That got me thinking. She was quite correct. Vincent had offered to help find me a dance partner several times. Not to mention the fact that he had been injured in the process of trying to stop a fight between me and Father. "Why are you so observant?" I asked.

"If it were not for my observations, I may have agreed to marry your friend and fallen into a life of complete misery," she joked. "Although, I suppose that if I had agreed, you would not have had to dance with me."

"Then you would have never had a friend who understands you," I finished her thought.

She nodded, "I would have been stuck with Louise."

"And I would have been stuck with Matthew."

"That would be a nightmare."

"He can be quite pleasant at times, you know."

"I never doubted that. However, I fear that he will always be bitter towards me."

"He usually comes to his senses. You may have to give him a few years of course."

"I may just die from the awkwardness before that happens," she giggled, before glancing at the clock on the desk. "I should go meet your sister. She wanted to show me the music room."

"You are sure to like it. It is much larger than the one at our estate."

She smiled at me before taking her leave. For a moment, I became caught up in her smile once again. Then I pulled myself out of it. "Why do I keep doing that?" I asked myself. I had been doing that quite a lot lately, for reasons I could not comprehend. As Matthew had once predicted, I did not even realize what was happening.

CHAPTER NINETEEN

Since arriving in London two weeks before, my life had been filled with nothing but happiness. It felt like I was in paradise. I did not have to worry about avoiding Matthew, or running after Louise. I had not felt such happiness in a long time. My days were filled with music and reading, and I could actually spend more than ten minutes with Jonathan every day.

It was so bizarre to think that I used to dislike the man. I used to loathe every minute spent in his presence, but now I could not wait to spend more time with him. I could not exactly comprehend why it was that way, but I did not really care.

At the moment, I was focusing on writing a letter to my family. I told them about how kind and considerate the Edwards family was, and how they were hosting a masquerade ball only a few days before our departure. I had to admit that I had missed my family quite a bit. I missed my dear old father in particular. Believe it or not, I actually missed hearing his endless complaints about life. I also missed the constant chaos that my adorable niece and nephew provided.

"Miss Caroline Gilmore has time for tea now, miss," Hannah informed me.

"Thank you, Hannah," I said, getting up from my desk and making my way out of the room.

"May I escort you somewhere, miss?" Mr. Brown asked, coming towards me.

"I suppose it would not hurt to have you escort me to the music room. I would not want to get lost."

He nodded and began to escort me down the corridor. I had become quite fond of Mr. Brown lately. At first he had appeared somewhat distant, however, with a bit of time, I realized that he was actually a very polite and considerate man. "Have we managed to bore you yet?" he asked.

"Not at all; I am quite enjoying my time here," I said.

"That is good to hear," he said. "How have you adjusted to having Hannah and Edith around?"

"It is nice not having to clean up after myself for once. Although I fear that I will be an utter slob by the time I return home."

He chuckled ever so slightly, "Well, here you are. If you need anything, I will be next door ensuring that our newest maid has not completely destroyed the room in which she was assigned to clean."

I nodded and entered the music room. Jonathan had been correct when he said that I would like it. It was bigger than any other music room I had ever seen. It had almost every instrument in existence, and in the centre of the room stood the most beautiful piano. It still seemed like a dream to be standing in such a room. My only hope was that I would not wake up back at home.

"Helene, it is good to see you," Caroline greeted me.

"I see that your aunt has finally given you enough time to enjoy yourself for a change," I teased her.

"Between the endless tea parties and tutoring my uncle's six-year-old niece, my life has been nothing but busy," she complained. "Do you normally have a problem getting your niece to cooperate with you?"

I nodded, "If she does not get her way, sometimes she throws a screaming fit."

She giggled, "Well, my young pupil threw a fit and tossed my sheet music all over the room."

"Children will be children. I am sure that I was intolerable at some point in my life."

"I suppose you are right. I imagine that we were all that way at some point," she said, sitting down on a sofa. "How do you like London so far?"

"It has been a bit overwhelming, but I have come to understand your family a bit more because of it," I replied, coming to sit across from her.

"I am pleased to hear that. I hope that you can see why my family is a little bit grumpy at times."

"Of course I do. Your father is always working. I feel sorry for Vincent. I cannot imagine him being the type of man to enjoy working all of the time. That must be why he is such a flirt."

"I believe you may just be correct," she agreed. "Have you heard anything about William lately?"

I nodded my head. "He has recently found a second job. He hopes to be able to rent a small house in a few months' time."

"It is horrible to think that it is because of my mother that he has to work so hard. I can hardly stand the thought that it is because of her that he had to leave again."

"He believes that you would be better off with someone who could support you."

She nodded in understanding. "Why does love have to be this way?"

"How do you even know if you're in love with someone?" I asked with a sudden curiosity.

"You know that you are in love when you cannot stop thinking about that person. You know it when you get excited at the thought of seeing him again. You know it when the very thought of him makes you smile," she said with a smile. "At least, that is how I knew."

Her words struck at my heart like a poisoned arrow. She had just described how I had been feeling lately towards Jonathan. It could not be that I was in love with him. I tried so hard to convince myself that it was only because I understood him more than anyone else, but the more I tried, the more I started to realize that I may have fallen for him after all.

"It cannot be," I thought. *"I do not even believe in love."*

Just then a servant entered the room. "Miss Gilmore, your mother wishes for you to join her and your aunt for tea out in the garden."

Caroline sighed. "Forgive me, Helene, but I have already refused one of Mother's demands today and I do not wish to anger her any further," she apologized, rushing out of the room.

I stayed seated there until I was certain that she was gone, before rushing out of the room and down the corridor to my room again. I was trying so hard to deny it. I tried to think of any excuse that would come to mind. How could I have fallen for him? The closest friend of the man I had rejected.

Finally, I could not deny it any longer. The truth was that I really could not stop thinking about him. When I looked at his eyes I could hardly tear myself away. I did get excited by the idea of seeing him, and the very thought of him made me smile. Everything that Caroline had said was true.

As I finally reached my room, tears began to fill my eyes. I slammed the door shut and rushed straight to my bed. I thanked God that Hannah and Edith were not in the room at the moment. The last thing that I wanted was for someone to see me cry. I was always afraid to let people see me cry because it made me feel so hideous. I buried my face in my hands and began to sob.

I could not believe that I had fallen in love with Jonathan Gilmore. The man of every woman's dreams. The man that before now I had considered one of the closest friends I had ever had. The man whom I had once claimed to despise. I had always thought that all of his admirers were nothing but delusional, empty-headed fools, but now I was one of them.

"Miss Hoffman, are you all right?" Mr. Brown asked, as he came into the room

"Leave me alone," I said between sobs.

"I know what you are going through," he said.

"I doubt that."

"You have fallen for the youngest of Mr. Gilmore's sons."

I dried my eyes on the sleeve of my dress and looked up at him. He was now standing next to my bed. "How did you know that?"

"I have spotted you with him quite a few times. It was clear to me that the two of you were in love with each other."

The tears began to flow again, "You are mistaken. He does not feel the same way. He does not even believe in love. I do not even know if it exists myself."

"Do you not care about your family?" he asked.

I nodded, "I care about my family very much, but what does that have to do with this?"

"Love is not defined by romantic feelings you know. Love can be between family members, friends, and even between you and the Great Creator himself."

In my life, my parents had never told me that they loved me, as it was not proper to display public signs of affection, but I always knew that they cared about me. I had never thought of it as love though, nor had I ever thought of the very real fact that God loved me. I had always only thought of it as toleration instead of love. Looking back at my life now, I realized that I had been loved my whole life. It had always been there; I had simply failed to see it.

"I wish that I could say that I loved Jonathan as a friend, but I am afraid that I cannot," I admitted, sitting up.

"I know that it is terrifying to suddenly realize that you love a person who may not feel the same way, but it is not the end of the world. You must live on as you always have before."

He was right. I had to keep moving forward. I had to pretend that nothing had happened, even if it killed me inside. "Thank you," I said with a weak smile. "Will you do me one more favour?"

"You need not worry. I will not tell anyone about this."

With a sigh of relief, I stood up and began to clean myself up. I put on a brave face and prepared myself to go out and face the world again. Something that my father always told me came to mind at that moment. *"You have endured far worse things,"* I remembered him telling me when I had sprained my ankle as a child.

I realized that I was being childish. I had endured far worse things than this. It was not as if I was having to watch my brother die before my eyes, or my father having his leg chopped off. This problem was nothing in comparison to those of my past, and I could not stop being strong now.

CHAPTER TWENTY

Over the past few days I had been attempting to take Miss Hoffman's advice and tried not to shut my family out of my life so much. Although, it was quite difficult at times like this. Our aunt had convinced us to spend some quality time with our cousins and so far it was nothing but a disaster. Thomas was so boring that he made me want to go back to sleep. At the moment, he was explaining his theory on dreams.

"Often times our inner most fears and feelings reveal themselves in our dreams," he explained.

I yawned, "Perhaps if you let me go to sleep right now, I can test out your theory."

Vincent and Anne laughed. "Does he normally sleep through breakfast?" Anne asked.

"Well, he normally does not get very much sleep. I always knew that his lack of sleep would catch up with him one day," he teased.

"You are hilarious, Vincent," I rolled my eyes.

"Perhaps Thomas will one day invent something that will enable me to see inside the brain of my younger brother."

Thomas dreamed of becoming an inventor and eventually coming up with something to make life easier. My brother liked to tease him about it a bit. I suppose that I did as well. "Perhaps he will invent a machine to count the number of women you have danced with. It would certainly make my life easier," I suggested with a slight chuckle.

Just then, our aunt entered the room. "What are you all talking about?" she asked.

"Jonathan was just about to tell us how many women Vincent has danced with," Anne said.

"On one occasion, I believe that I counted almost ten different women. That is not even counting all of the women he flirts with in between dances."

Vincent blushed deep red, "I think you may be exaggerating."

"I am sure that you have a lot of admirers as well Jonathan," Aunt Josephine joined in.

"Every girl in Portsmouth would love to dance with him and yet he has only danced with one of them," Vincent complained.

"The woman I danced with happened to hate me, actually," I corrected him.

"Why on earth did you dance with a woman who hated you?" Anne asked.

"I was tired of Vincent nagging me."

"I was only nagging him because Mother was nagging me."

"You are not a very close family are you?"

"I blame that on Mother as well. We broke one vase as children and she never let us interact with each other again."

"I know that your mother is strict, but I am sure that she only wants what is best for you," Aunt Josephine defended.

"Mother wants what is best for herself. She cares not for how we feel," I insisted. The room fell silent for a long time before I decided to take my leave. Unfortunately, Vincent followed me out.

"How do you do it?" he asked.

"Do what?"

"How do you manage to speak so boldly without regretting it?"

I shrugged, "The truth may hurt, but it does make people listen. How do you think I have been able to keep Mother from forcing me into an arranged marriage?"

He stayed quiet until we reached my bedroom. "Perhaps I should try speaking like that the next time she brings up my so-called fiancée."

I plopped myself down onto one of the sofas in my room, "You really do not want to marry her, do you?"

"It is bad enough that I will have to take over Father's position. I should at least be able to marry someone I actually love," he replied, sitting down on the sofa next to me.

"How do you even know if you are in love?" I wondered with a sudden, unexplainable curiosity.

"I do not actually have any personal experience with love, but I have heard about it from other people," he explained. "Apparently you know that you are in love when you cannot stop thinking about a person, and when you suddenly find yourself wanting to see her more. I suppose you would know it when you cannot help but be taken in by something simple like her smile."

"What?" It felt as if my mind had just broken into a thousand pieces. That was almost exactly how I had been feeling towards Miss Hoffman. It could not possibly be that I was in love with her. Love did not exist after all.

Vincent looked at me strangely, "What is wrong?"

"Nothing," I denied, trying very hard to convince myself, as well as my brother.

His eyes widened suddenly, "Are you in love with someone?"

"I am most certainly not," I said sternly, trying to keep my composure.

"It is wonderful that you have finally found someone! Why are you denying it?" he said, a small grin forming on his face.

"Because I do not even believe in love!" I snapped at him.

I could clearly tell that he was quite surprised by this. "Why would you not believe in love?" he asked.

"Why would I believe in it? There has never been any in my life. Our own parents hate each other."

He did not know what to say after that. He knew that I was right, although often times he hated to admit it. "How long have you felt this way?" he asked.

I sighed, "Many years."

"Why did you not tell anyone?" he asked.

"It is not exactly something I want everyone to know. I would have a mob of angry women after me."

"Is this the reason why you never dance?"

I nodded. "It would seem that you do not need Thomas to create a machine to look inside my mind after all."

"Let me get this straight. You are in love with the woman you danced with at the ball?"

"I am not in love with her!" I exclaimed.

"Just because our parents hate each other does not mean that love does not exist. If love never existed, then why did God sacrifice his only son so that our sins could be forgiven? There is more than one type of love."

"Like what?"

"There is the love between family members. Aunt Josephine loves us quite a bit," he gave an example.

"Is that why she was pinching our cheeks yesterday?"

"Yes, that is her way of showing how precious we are to her."

"That is different. She does not know us that well."

"I do not know you that well either," he noted. I looked at him with surprise. My older brother loved me? I was not exactly sure whether to be happy or disgusted. "Why do you think that I always came to talk to you even when I knew that you would just shut me out again?"

"It is just like she said," I thought. Despite still processing the fact that my brother actually loved me, I could not help but return to the matter at hand. I could scarcely believe that I had actually managed to fall in love with Miss Hoffman. The very woman whom I had once thought to be cold-hearted. The very woman whom I had despised for humiliating my friend. It would seem that Matthew had actually been correct when he said that I would not even know it if I was in love with someone.

That was when something horrible dawned on me. I was in love with the woman who had broken Matthew's heart. He would be furious with me if he ever discovered this. I could only imagine what his fiery temper would cause him to do.

"Now, are you going to tell me the name of the lucky woman?"

"I cannot."

"Why not?"

"Nothing can ever happen between us."

"What do you mean?"

"Mother would never allow it."

"Who knows what will happen. Maybe if you yell at her enough she will allow it," he joked. Even if Mother did allow it, I knew that Miss Hoffman did not believe in love herself. I would simply have to pretend that nothing had happened and continue on with my life. It might tear me apart inside, but I felt that it was necessary.

CHAPTER TWENTY-ONE

Just when I thought that nothing could ruin my time here in London, things had to become complicated. Being near Jonathan was now more awkward than ever. It seemed like neither of us could think of anything to say. We had accidentally bumped into each other in the hallway a couple of days before and I had the hardest time concentrating on anything. All I could do was stare into his eyes.

I had noticed that he seemed to be distracted by something; however, my only thought was that he'd had another fight with his mother. I never suspected that it might be something else. I honestly thought that my newly discovered feelings were one sided.

Just then, a knock came at my door. "I shall get it," Edith said, as she went to open the door. It was Miss Edwards.

"Is Miss Hoffman ready?" she asked.

Miss Edwards had offered to take me into London to look for a new dress for the ball. I did have a bit of money, but I feared that I would not be able to afford anything extravagant. My primary reason for accepting her offer was so that I could look around a bit. I knew that I would never return to London, so I wanted to make the most of this trip and see all that I could.

"We had a bit of a problem waking her up, but she is ready now," Edith told her, motioning for me to come.

She smiled at me as I came out from the bedroom. "Mr. Brown has agreed to accompany us, and the carriage is waiting for us as we speak."

I smiled slightly at Mr. Brown, who was peeking around the corner. "Then let us get going."

Mr. Brown escorted us through the long maze of corridors, down a couple flights of stairs, and to the door. The carriage was the fanciest that I had ever seen. Sitting down onto its rich velvet seats, I felt a bit undeserving of the privilege and feared that I would stick out like a sore thumb in London.

"Are you not accustomed to riding in a carriage like this?" she asked, noticing my uneasiness.

Technically, my family's carriage did not have a roof of any sort and was quite uncomfortable for me on the hottest days. "Not quite," I admitted.

"So, what do the women of Portsmouth think about my two cousins, Vincent and Jonathan?" she asked.

"Well, Vincent is considered the town flirt. Every woman who comes to my mind would jump at the chance to spend even a minute with him."

She giggled slightly, "And what about Jonathan?"

I was unsure of what to tell her initially. I finally decided to simply tell her how they really saw him. "Most of the women are hypnotized by his dashing good looks, but think that he is arrogant."

"Why?"

"He never dances with anyone."

"Vincent told me that he danced with one woman."

"I have heard that as well, although no one knows who she is."

"She must not mean very much to him. If she did, he would have told us her name."

My heart sank when she said that. She was probably right; I did not mean that much to him. I tried so hard not to care, but at times I could not help it.

"At which shop did you wish to stop?" Mr. Brown asked.

"I was hoping to stop at my favourite dress shop," she said, and then turned to me. "Mr. Pike's Dress Emporium has the most wonderful gowns in all of London!"

"I look forward to seeing them."

We chatted about the latest style of gowns for a while before we arrived at a fancy-looking shop. Mr. Brown stepped out and helped us out of the carriage and led us into the shop. There were quite a few young women close to my age in the shop, looking at gowns of every colour and size. In all my life, I had never seen so many beautiful dresses in one place. The only problem was that I could not afford any of them. All of the dresses were very expensive. I looked around and pretended that I could afford them. The last thing I wanted was to draw attention to myself among these high-society women.

"Have you found any that you like?" Anne asked, coming up behind me.

"It is such a hard decision. There are so many to choose from."

"Perhaps I can help you," she suggested. "What is your favourite colour?"

"I am quite fond of red."

She immediately called the shop owner over, "Bring my friend the most beautiful red dress that you can find."

The shop owner ran into the back of the shop and returned with a breath-taking red satin dress with white trim. "It is beautiful," I admitted.

"We will take this one as well as the lilac one near the counter," she said, pointing to the dress that she wanted.

"As you wish, milady," the shop owner said, rushing over to get the dress.

"That dress is more expensive than the one you are buying. I could never afford it," I whispered.

"That is why I am going to purchase it for you," she said with a giggle. "You need not worry about owing me."

I was speechless. No one had ever done something like this for me. I was having a troublesome time figuring out why she would do such a selfless thing. I had done nothing for her and yet she had treated me so kindly and chatted with me as if we were old friends. I had to admit that it was nice to be able to talk to someone who was not constantly trying to outshine me.

Once we were finished at the dress shop, and had re-entered the carriage, I decided to question her. "May I ask why you purchased such an extravagant dress for me?"

She was quiet for a moment, "I have never had a real friend before. There have been many women who have claimed to be my friend, but they only pretended to be my friend because of who my father is. I only wanted to do something nice for you since you have been so nice to me."

"I too have never had a real friend. There is a girl back in Portsmouth who claims to be my friend. However, she likes to think that she is better than me at everything,"

She looked slightly surprised. "It would seem that we have a bit in common, even though we come from completely different parts of the world."

I nodded in agreement. "I have to admit that, when I first arrived here, I was expecting to meet a family of snobby nobles who thought they were better than me, but now that I have met you and your family, I see that not all nobles are bad."

"I am glad to hear that," she smiled widely. We rode for a short while in silence before she spoke again. "If you ever feel like venting to someone about your so-called friend in Portsmouth, you could write me a letter. I would not mind."

"Perhaps I will take you up on your offer sometime," I said, smiling back at her.

CHAPTER TWENTY-TWO

I could hardly believe that in three days we would be returning home. It seemed like just yesterday we had arrived. So much had happened over the month that we had been in London. I was secretly not looking forward to going back home. Knowing that I had fallen in love with the woman who had broken Matthew's heart would make things extremely awkward for me. I had told him so many lies about what had happened. How would I ever be able to explain the situation to him?

"I wonder which one of these masked men is my younger brother?" Vincent joked as he walked up beside me.

The only good part about this ball was that everyone wore masks, ensuring that no one could identify you. Although, it was rather easy to identify my brother with his mask. "I am sorry, I thought that I heard my elder brother speaking to me, and yet the only thing I see is a gigantic bird," I teased.

"I was not aware that you had a sense of humour," he commented.

"I have always had a sense of humour. The only issue is that many fail to notice it."

"I can assume that you will not be dancing tonight either."

I rolled my eyes. "Of course not. But with your injured arm keeping you off the floor, it will be quite boring ... what with not being able to count the number of women with whom you dance."

"I am sorry to disappoint you. Perhaps you should take my place."

"There is no way that I am dancing with ten different women."

He chuckled, "Well, if we are not planning on dancing, we should go find Thomas and see what kind of invention he has created."

We began to make our way through the tightly packed crowd to the other side of the ballroom. As we chatted on our way, we accidentally bumped into a lovely woman. "We are so sorry, ma'am. Are you all right?" Vincent apologized.

"I am fine, thank you," said a very familiar voice.

"Miss Hoffman, is that you?" Vincent asked. I was certain that my eyes would pop out of their sockets at that moment.

"I am not quite certain. I hardly recognize myself," she said. "That is an interesting mask you are wearing."

Vincent blushed with embarrassment. "My aunt made me wear it."

She giggled slightly, "I would not worry too much. Your cousin is wearing one with antlers."

"Really?" he asked.

She nodded, "I just saw him dancing with a peacock."

Vincent chuckled, "I hope that he did not bore her."

"I do not believe that anyone would become bored with him, considering the way he dances," she said. "Now if you will excuse me, I need to find your sister."

"I am guessing that our ridiculous cousin is not very good at dancing," I noted, as I watched her disappear.

"Poor woman," he stated.

"You should have jumped in and saved her," I teased.

He rolled his eyes, "I am not that obsessed."

We continued on our way towards Thomas. Just as Miss Hoffman had said, he was wearing a mask with antlers. "We heard that you were caught dancing with a peacock," Vincent said, a playful smile forming on his lips.

"She was quite beautiful," he replied with enthusiasm. "Although, she seemed to be distracted by these gigantic antlers of mine."

"Sadly you are not the only one with a horrible mask," Vincent complained.

"Yours is actually worse than mine," he snivelled.

"It is not!"

"It is so!"

After a while of listening to them argue back and forth, I lost interest and decided to walk around the ballroom to see if there was anyone else wearing a hideous mask. I managed to spot one elephant and even another man wearing a bird beak. There were a lot of masks with feathers attached and quite a few with jewels of every colour.

That was when I noticed Miss Hoffman. She was standing outside on the balcony all alone, with her mask in her hand. She appeared to be enjoying the ball just as much as I was. I fought with myself over whether or not to go and join her. There was a part of me that felt like I ought to stay away from her, and then there was a part of me that wanted the complete opposite.

I finally walked out and stood beside her, after deciding that I could not fight the urge. "From the looks of it, you are enjoying the ball just as much as I am," I commented.

She looked over at me and smiled weakly. "I fear that you are correct. Although seeing all of the strange masks has been quite entertaining."

"Indeed it has," I agreed. "Did you see the man with the elephant mask?"

She giggled and nodded. "What is it with all of the animal masks?"

"That would be my aunt's personal touch."

"I see that you managed to escape the fate of your brother," she said, gesturing to my dark, nondescript mask selection.

"The bird beak of his is quite ridiculous is it not?"

"I was trying so hard not to laugh in front of him," she admitted.

We stood there in silence for quite some time. No matter how hard I tried to pretend that nothing had happened, it felt like everything had changed between us. I broke the silence. "For a moment back there, I nearly mistook you for a noble woman."

"You can blame the dress for that. I was planning on getting a dress that better befitted a dull doorknob; however, Anne insisted that I get this one."

"I am glad that she talked you into it. You do look very beautiful."

"I suppose that the dress is very beautiful, but…"

"I was not referring to the dress," I interrupted.

"You think I am beautiful?" she asked.

I was at a loss for words. She seemed quite surprised by what I had said; however, she did not seem to be objecting as much as she usually did. For a moment, a bit of hope sparked inside me. Perhaps she had changed her mind about love as well? Despite the doubt clouding my judgement, I made up my mind once and for all. I pulled off my mask, feeling the cool night air on my cheeks.

"You are the most beautiful woman I have ever seen. Not only on the outside, but on the inside as well."

As she turned to face me, I spotted a slight blush on her face. "Do you really mean it?" she asked, a smile forming on her lips once again.

I turned to face her as well. "I really do."

We stood there for what seemed to be forever, just looking at each other. My heart began to race like never before. The palms of my hands became sweaty. Before I could stop myself, I was moving closer to her, and then our lips met.

It was a better experience than I had ever imagined. Her lips were soft and smooth. The smell of her fragrant perfume flooded my senses. Her skin felt refreshingly cold against my own. For a mere moment, I forgot all about where I was. Then it all came crashing back down on me, as I realized exactly what I was doing.

I pulled away suddenly and stepped back. She seemed surprised at first, but then a smile surfaced. "Whatever happened to not believing in love?" she asked.

"I suppose you could say that I had my eyes opened," I replied. "What about you?"

She giggled slightly, "I had my eyes opened as well."

I could not believe my ears. She had changed her mind as well? I could not express just how relieved I was to hear her say that. However, my relief soon disappeared when I saw the look of worry on Miss Hoffman's face. "What is wrong?" I asked her.

"Both your mother and Matthew will be furious when they learn of this."

"Who says that they have to find out?" I asked. She looked at me with a look of confusion. "It would only be one more secret to keep."

"No one has discovered the other secrets yet, so I suppose that it could work."

"It will be our secret," I said with a slight grin. "Now, I do not suppose that you would care to dance with me?"

"That depends. Is there anything you wish to interrogate me about?" she teased, replacing her mask.

"As a matter of fact there is. I would like to interrogate you regarding your feelings for me."

"All right, but then I get to interrogate you as well."

With a small chuckle, I donned my mask as well, and escorted her back into the crowd. Perhaps this ball would not be entirely awful after all.

CHAPTER
TWENTY-THREE

The last three days in London
had been bittersweet. I would miss London very much. The Edwards
had been very kind and considerate of me. I had arrived expecting
them to be snobby, and left with the regret of never being able to see
them again. Although I did not leave without promising to write to
Anne. It would be nice to have a real friend with whom to correspond.

I looked around at my three travelling companions. Mrs. Gilmore
had insisted that Caroline ride with her this time, and so I had ended
up riding with Vincent, Jonathan, and Mr. Gilmore. Most of the
journey had gone well. However, it had started to go downhill when
Vincent had fallen asleep. I could not believe that it was possible for
someone to snore louder than my father.

"Did you enjoy your time in London, Miss Hoffman?" Mr.
Gilmore asked.

I nodded, "It was wonderful, but all good things must come to an
end I am afraid."

"You are quite right," he agreed. "I am sure that your family will
be wanting to hear about your trip."

I was actually not looking forward to that part. I would have to
leave out all of the parts about Jonathan when telling them of my

trip. It pained me to leave them out of this part of my life, but I supposed that it had to be kept a secret. "My father might not be too interested, but I am sure that my mother will be."

"Your mother always did seem a bit more enthusiastic," he remarked.

"I assure you that my father is enthusiastic about things as well. I have never seen anyone get as excited about a new book as he does."

"If you ask me, he sounds a bit like Jonathan," Vincent said with a yawn, as he opened his eyes and looked around.

"Perhaps you should run away and join a circus. They would surely find a good use for your sense of humour," Jonathan retorted.

I laughed. "Do they always do this?"

"Unfortunately so," Mr. Gilmore said with a sigh.

I spotted my house then, as we rounded the corner. While I had immensely enjoyed the privileges at the Edwards' manor, I was happy to return to my quaint little house. Having a bunch of servants following me around, waiting on me hand and foot, had become overwhelming, and I was looking forward to being able to clean up after myself once again.

As we came to a stop in front of the house, I quickly glanced at Jonathan, and then stepped out of the carriage. "Send our regards to your family," Mr. Gilmore called, as a servant handed me my suitcase.

"I certainly will," I replied. With the nod of his head, the carriage turned around and pulled out. As soon as I could no longer see them, I walked up to the door and turned the handle. My mother stood in front of the stairs, as if she had been waiting for hours.

"My sweet little Helene has returned!" my mother exclaimed, as she threw her arms around me in a warm embrace.

"I missed you too, Mama," I replied, putting down my suitcase and returning the hug.

"How was your trip?" she asked, as she released me from her arms.

"It was very nice, but a bit overwhelming. By the end of it, I actually missed having to clean up after myself," I explained with a small giggle. "Where is Papa?"

She rolled her eyes. "He is in the study with his nose glued to another book. I do not believe he is even aware that you have returned."

With a big grin, I approached the study and knocked on the door. "I am nearly finished, Johanna!" came the reply.

I opened the door and peered inside. "It must be an interesting book."

He looked up when he heard my voice. "Dornröschen has returned," he said, with one of his rare smiles.

I walked over to him and gave him a quick hug. "Mr. Gilmore sends his regards."

"I am surprised that he did not follow you in."

"He would have, except Mrs. Gilmore had a headache and insisted on going straight home," I explained.

He shook his head. "That woman always seems to have a headache."

Suddenly, Giselle came rushing into the room. "Aunt Helene!" she exclaimed.

I gathered her into my arms. "You will never know how much I missed seeing your adorable face every day."

She smiled with delight. "Did you bring me anything?"

"Giselle, let your aunt breathe for a moment before you start asking her if she brought you anything," Alexander complained, coming into the room with Henry.

"Actually I brought something back for both you *and* Henry."

"What are they?"

"If you go fetch my suitcase, I will show you." I set her down on the floor and watched her run off. Minutes later she returned, pulling my suitcase behind her. I took it from her and opened it up. "I have a new toy train for Henry."

Henry gurgled with delight when I handed him the train. "You did not have to get them anything you know," Alexander insisted.

"I would not be a very good aunt if I did not get them anything, and besides, I really do not mind spending my money on them. There was not much that I really wanted anyway."

"What did you get me?" Giselle interrupted.

I dug into my suitcase and grabbed a brand new doll from under one of my dresses. "Will this do?" I asked, handing her the doll.

"She is beautiful!" Giselle exclaimed, hugging her tightly.

"You have nothing for your favourite brother?" Alexander teased.

"I simply do not think that you would look good in a dress," I joked.

He pulled a face at me. "Very funny."

It was good to be home again. Living in London for a month with the Edwards had taught me to appreciate what I have. Wealth and nobility was not everything that I had imagined. Even though my life involved a lot more work, I would never change it when it came to family.

"You mentioned that Mr. Gilmore's sister was throwing a masquerade ball in your letter. How did that turn out?" Father asked.

I blushed at the very thought of it. I could still not believe that Jonathan had actually kissed me. It would seem that he had changed his mind at nearly the same time I had. "It was wonderful," I said. I had to admit that I was slightly uncertain of what lay ahead. Mrs. Gilmore would never accept me and I did not expect her to. I finally knew how it felt to love someone that you could never be with. It was only one more thing that I had in common with Caroline.

In addition to this, I was quite worried about how Jonathan and Matthew's friendship would fare if Matthew ever discovered what had happened. Matthew was quite prone to doing reckless things when upset, and after seeing how he acted when I broke his heart, I was afraid to see what he might be like when he uncovered the truth. A question began to float around my head like an annoying fly: What exactly would he do when he found out?

CHAPTER
TWENTY-FOUR

The sun beat down on my face as I rode like never before. Tybalt was one of the fastest horses my family had ever seen. His name suited his personality quite well, for he was quite aggressive, but at the same time he was very loyal. At times I considered him to be my best friend. I could tell him anything without fear that he would lose his temper.

You may think that it sounds silly to talk to a horse, but I found that it helped me calm down after an encounter with my mother or Matthew. I had told him about what had happened in London and how I had kissed Miss Hoffman. I had even asked him what I should do about Matthew, but as you can imagine, horses are terrible at giving advice.

"There you are!" a voice said all of a sudden.

I brought Tybalt to an abrupt halt when I saw someone just ahead of me. At first I could not recognize who it was, but then I caught a glimpse of his face and knew immediately. "Matthew?" I asked. "What on earth are you doing out here?"

"Excuse me for wanting to visit my friend, whom I have not seen in a month," he defended himself.

"Sorry," I apologized.

"How was your trip?"

"It was all right, I suppose."

"What were your cousins like?"

"Thomas was a bit strange, but Anne was fairly decent."

"What was Miss Hoffman like?" he asked nervously.

I had been expecting him to ask that. Luckily, I already knew exactly what to tell him. "I did not really pay that much attention to her," I lied.

He rolled his eyes. "I should have guessed that. You could not care less about her."

He did not know just how wrong he was. I had come to care about her a lot over the past couple of months. Sadly I could not tell him that for fear of his temper. "She seemed to be enjoying herself," I informed him.

"I cannot believe that I was so obsessed with her not too long ago," he complained. "I wish that you had stopped me from proposing to her that day."

At first I had felt the same way. However, if I had stopped him, I would not have confronted her, and in the end, would not have fallen for her. Somehow I did not find myself regretting what had happened, even though I knew that Matthew would be furious.

"If I had done that, you would have just gotten angry at me."

"You are probably right," he agreed. "How is your brother's arm?"

"He has recovered quite a bit. Although, my mother treats him like he cannot do anything for himself. I would not be surprised if she started spoon feeding him."

"That would certainly be a sight to see," he chuckled.

"Indeed it would," I replied, "I suppose that I should get back to the house."

"I will meet you there," he said, briefly getting a head start before I galloped past, leaving him in a cloud of dust. "Show off!" he yelled after me.

As soon as I arrived at the stables, I quickly dismounted and left the servants to untack Tybalt. By the time I had reached the front door, Matthew had caught up with me. "Master Jonathan, your mother is looking for you," a servant notified me as we made our way upstairs.

I groaned, "What does she want now?"

"I believe she has received word from Mrs. Parker in Southampton," he notified me.

I stopped dead in my tracks. "You may tell her that I have been eaten by wild animals and that my funeral will be held in a week from now."

The servant stared at me with a look of uncertainty for a moment. "As you wish," he said with a nod before continuing on his way.

"Who is Mrs. Parker?" Matthew asked as we continued our way up the stairs.

"A friend of my mother's," I explained. "She has a daughter who is around my age."

"I thought that she wanted you to marry Mrs. Bellinger's daughter."

"I managed to talk her out of that one."

He nodded his head in understanding. "Now she is trying to marry you off to Mrs. Parker's daughter instead."

"You are starting to catch on to these things."

"Hello, little brother," Vincent greeted me, sneaking up from behind and ruffling my hair.

"Yes, it is nice to see you too," I said. "What do you want?"

"I was simply wondering why Mother suddenly thinks that you are dead."

"She actually believed it?" Matthew asked in shock.

He shrugged, "I just saw her rush over to Father's study. She was mumbling something about a funeral."

"I instructed one of the servants to tell her that I had been killed."

"Why would you do that?" he asked.

"She received word from Mrs. Parker in Southampton."

"That would explain it," he said, winking at me. "Of course you do not want to marry *her*," he called as he went on his way

"When did you start getting along with your brother?"

"You would be surprised what can happen in a month," I said, leaving him standing there speechless. I could only wish to comprehend what was going through his head at that moment. Although, I assumed that he was wondering what on earth had happened to make me get along with Vincent. "If only he knew," I mumbled to myself.

CHAPTER
TWENTY-FIVE

Life had returned to normal
for me. I would wake up later than I ought to thanks to a certain
annoying brother of mine. Then I would rush to get dressed and
head down to get to work. My daily chores consisted of sweeping
the floors, beating out the rugs, and taking care of Giselle and Henry
when Charlotte was unable to do so.

This morning I had been instructed to go feed the horses while
Alexander prepared the carriage. When I asked them where we
were going, they would change the topic. I found this quite unusual,
because normally someone notified me if we were going somewhere.
I had a feeling that wherever we were going, something horrible
would happen.

I knew that my father would never lie to me on purpose, so I
decided to see if he would tell me. He was reclined on his chair in
the living room, reading a book. I sat down on the armrest beside
him and stayed there until he looked up. "May I help you, my dear?"
he asked.

"Is there a reason why nobody wants me to know where we are
going?" I asked him. "I have a feeling that it is because we are going
to be visiting the Caldwell manor."

"I am afraid that you are correct," he sighed and set down his book. "While you were gone, Mr. Caldwell made plans for a fishing derby. It is being held in about an hour and your brother wishes to take part," he explained.

The colour drained out of my face. This would be the first time I had encountered the Caldwells since my return. Without a doubt, Matthew would still be bitter towards me. I cringed at the very thought of spending three whole hours being stared at by him. "Do we have to go?" I asked.

He nodded his head, "If you do not want to watch, I am sure that Mr. Caldwell would not mind if you explored the estate."

I gave in. "All right."

He kissed the top of my head. "You should go fix your hair and change into a better dress. We will be leaving as soon as I finish the last chapter of my book."

I nodded and trudged up into my room. I tried so hard to think positively. Perhaps Matthew would be too busy fishing to notice me. Perhaps I could go inside the house and find a place to hide. Perhaps I would turn invisible and no one would even see me. I was desperate to find a way to escape.

As I was searching through my wardrobe, looking for an appropriate dress to wear, I remembered that Jonathan would most likely be there as well. All of a sudden, I was excited to go see him. I grabbed a light purple dress and began to change out of the dress I was wearing and into the clean one. Then I began to brush and style my hair. Under normal circumstances, I preferred my hair to be left hanging, but I knew that Mother would throw a fit if I did not style my hair for the occasion.

"Are you ready?" Father called.

"Yes, Papa!" I exclaimed, rushing out of the room and down the stairs. "Do you have your cane?" I asked.

He held it up, to show me that he did have it, before using it to nudge me out of the house. "Unless you wish to be late, let us get going," he said, hurrying me into the carriage.

"I have known you for twenty-four years and we have rarely been late for anything. Instead we usually end up arriving half an hour early," Alexander complained.

Father was known to be quite impatient. His greatest fear seemed to be that we would be late on occasions like this. Eventually, he must have come to the conclusion that if we always arrived half an hour early we would never be late. That was simply the way that he was.

As we pulled out, I began to think about Louise. I had not left on the best terms with her, and I was worried to a certain extent. Normally she forgets these things with time, but when she did not, she was known to start vicious rumours about people.

I had heard that she was officially engaged to James Caldwell. I did not know the exact details, but according to what I had heard from my mother, James had proposed to her only two weeks after I had left. The thought of her being the sister-in-law to Matthew only further convinced me to stay away from her.

It filled me with dread to think about how their marriage would fare. Louise was easily distracted by handsome men, and in all honesty, I could imagine her being unfaithful to James. She had nearly forgotten about him when she had met Mr. Johnson. For once in my life, I actually found myself feeling a bit sorry for James.

"Prepare yourself," Alexander teased. "We are nearly there."

I rolled my eyes. "I have eyes as well, Alexander." I felt a lump in my throat as we pulled up at the Caldwell manor. I could not help but wonder what misfortunes I would be put through today. The last time that I had been here, Matthew had proposed to me. I doubted that would happen again, for Matthew's feelings towards me had surely changed since then.

I stepped out of the carriage and looked around. There was already a large crowd of people assembled across the estate. I could spot all of the Gilmores except Jonathan, which disappointed me greatly, but I was quite pleased to not find Matthew anywhere among the crowd.

"Helene!" someone called out to me all of a sudden. To my surprise, it was none other than Louise. "I am so glad that you are back!"

"It is nice to see that I was missed," I said with a smile.

"Of course I missed you. I had no one to talk to while you were gone," she replied.

"Did you not have James to talk to? I heard that he finally proposed to you."

"Indeed he did!" she squealed with delight as she showed me her fancy engagement ring. "The wedding is to be held in the summer; although an official date has not yet been chosen."

"I wish you my congratulations. I do hope that you two will be happy."

"Now I just need to find you a husband," she teased.

I sighed, "Have you not given up on that?"

She shook her head. "Are you sure that you are not interested in Matthew Caldwell? You would inherit this entire estate after the passing of the reverend."

"I could not care less about wealth. You really must accept that I am not the least bit interested in him."

"If everyone would follow me to the pond, we will get the fishing derby under way!" Mr. Caldwell called.

Before I could blink an eye, Louise had rushed off after James. With an irritated sigh, I began to make my way down to the pond, where I soon found my father standing under a shady tree, talking to Mr. Abbott and Mr. Caldwell.

"Miss Hoffman, it is a pleasure to see you again," Mr. Abbott greeted me. "How was your time in London?"

"It was quite refreshing. I have never seen a place quite as large," I replied.

"I fear that this must be a nightmare compared to your time there," Mr. Caldwell said. "As I recall, you are not particularly fond of fishing."

"I am afraid that I am not interested in many outdoor activities, aside from walking that is."

"If that is the case, then please feel free to walk about the estate. I am sure that you will find something interesting along the way."

"You are too kind," I thanked him with a smile, before making my way across the grounds and into the forest. The trails were without a doubt meant for riding, but I doubted that anyone would be out riding at a time like this. Everyone was far too engrossed in fishing to do anything else. The mere thought of handling a slimy, disgusting fish was completely revolting to me.

As I was walking along, someone suddenly grabbed hold of my hand. I stopped and swung my head around to see Jonathan standing right behind me. "What are you doing all the way out here?" he asked.

"Mr. Caldwell gave me permission to explore a bit," I explained with a smile. "I thought that I would try to find something with which to occupy myself."

"I fear that there is not much that would interest you here, besides the walking trails. Normally when I am with Matthew, I go for a horse-back ride, but seeing that you do not like riding..."

"The problem is not that I dislike riding," I corrected him. "The problem is that I have never actually ridden a horse."

"You have never ridden a horse?" he asked in disbelief.

I shook my head. "My father never taught me how to. He believes that his leg prevents him from riding."

"Well then, perhaps one day I will have to teach you."

"I would like that very much," I replied.

We walked along the forest trails for quite some time. We did not speak at all, but somehow just being close to him made me feel at peace. When I was with him, I seemed to forget all about the burden of my painful memories. They remained, but became more bearable.

After a while, we came to a stop under an enormous tree. From one of its thick branches, there hung a wooden swing, and halfway up the tree there was a landing, which held some book and a few toys. I immediately recognized one of them as Matthew's slingshot from the day of my arrival.

"I did not think that it was still here," Jonathan said.

It certainly looked like it would have been fun for a child. Giselle surely would have loved to play here, for she was quite fond of climbing trees, much to the dismay of her mother. "I can assume that you and Matthew used to play here as children?"

He nodded. "I fell once and broke my arm, but it was still fun to climb up onto its branches."

"I suppose that your mother did not let you climb trees after that."

He grinned. "You know me too well."

I giggled, "I find it hard to believe that I once hated you."

"And I find it hard to believe that I managed to fall for such a beautiful and intelligent woman."

I blushed deep red. "I honestly do not think I merit such compliments."

He inched closer, getting ready to kiss me again. "You have no idea just how beautiful you are."

He pressed his warm lips against mine. I could not help but blush when he kissed me. I truly was not used to it; however, I hoped that I would have many opportunities to become accustomed. It was one of the more pleasant things that I had experienced. We slowly broke apart and stood there, looking into each other's eyes.

The more that I looked at him, the more that I had to thank God for bringing him into my life. I was incredibly lucky to be standing there with him. There were probably dozens of women who would love to be in my shoes. To be honest, I was worried about what would happen if they ever found out. Surely, there would be quite a few women who would be jealous.

Just then, I saw someone hiding behind a tree nearby. My eyes widened in shock as I caught a glance of the person's face. It was the man whom I had rejected and left heartbroken all of those months ago. The world came crashing down in front of me. All of the secrets that we had tried to keep from him were now evident.

"What is wrong?" Jonathan asked, turning to see what I was looking at. He caught on just as Matthew went racing off. He started to go after him, but stopped short and glanced back at me.

"You should go after him," I told him.

"I will see you soon," he promised, as he took off into the woods.

Tears began to stream down my face when I heard Matthew yelling from a distance. I could tell that Jonathan was trying to explain, but Matthew was not giving him the chance. He was clearly too upset to listen to anyone; although I was thankful that he had run off instead of doing something reckless.

I glanced at the enormous tree in front of me and felt guilty. I felt that this was my fault. I was the one who had asked Jonathan to keep everything a secret after all. I could not bear to think that he might lose his closest friend because of me, but I felt powerless. There was nothing that I could do to fix this. I felt like giving up.

That was when an idea came to mind. There was one way that I could help; however, I felt that I should let Matthew calm down for a few days before attempting it. My only hope was that it would help in some way instead of making things worse.

CHAPTER TWENTY-SIX

Weeks passed and I did not see Matthew at all. Normally I would have enjoyed spending a few weeks without him, but knowing that he was upset only made me feel guilty. I did not regret falling in love with Miss Hoffman, but I found myself wondering what would have happened if I had just told him why she had turned down his proposal. Although, if I had told him, I fear that she would have hated me even more.

It felt like I was caught between a rock and a hard place. I did not want to lose her, but I also did not want to lose my closest friend. I had absolutely no clue what I could do that would fix this problem. All I could do was pray that he would calm down and let me explain. I could not imagine what he was thinking; however, I was quite certain that it made me look like some sort of horrible monster.

"Jonathan, are you ready yet?" Vincent asked from the other side of my door.

"As ready as I can get," I replied, swinging open the door and joining my siblings in the hallway.

Today my father was meeting with the church council, which included the Caldwells. It would surely be awkward between me, Matthew, and Miss Hoffman. However, I hoped that my father would discuss something interesting for a change, so that I could distract myself.

"What is wrong? I thought that you would be more enthusiastic about seeing your friend. You have not had the chance to visit with him properly since we returned from London," Caroline commented.

"Matthew and I are not on the best terms right now," I informed them.

"What happened?" Vincent asked.

"We had a dispute a couple of weeks ago. I am not even certain if we are friends anymore."

"Have you tried talking to him?" she asked.

"He does not listen," I replied with a nod. "He is likely to never speak to me again."

"It is fortunate that Father has given us permission to miss the meeting then."

"Speaking of that, I should get going," Caroline said, beginning to make her way towards the music room. Without a doubt she was planning on spending her time with Miss Hoffman. At least I knew where I could find her. I hoped to sneak over to see her when she was done with my sister.

"Will you be spending the day in the library as usual?" Vincent asked as I started towards the very place of which he spoke.

I rolled my eyes, "Where else would I go?"

"I thought that you might be going off to see Miss Hoffman?"

I stopped dead in my tracks. "Why would I want to see her?"

"Do not be coy with me. I saw you with her on the balcony in London."

I blushed with embarrassment. "Did anyone else take notice?"

"You need not worry. No one else did," he assured me.

I breathed a sigh of relief and thanked God that it was not my mother, "If you tell anyone about that, I will ensure that no woman ever wants to dance with you again."

He chuckled, "I do not see why you insist on being so secretive about it. She is a wonderful woman and I am certain that Father would approve of her."

"That is not why I am being so secretive." And with that I hurried down the corridor and into the library. I walked about the library and searched for a book with which to occupy myself for the day. I was drawn to a certain book called *The Tenant of Wildfell Hall*.

The story revolved around a young woman named Helen Huntingdon, and a man named Gilbert Markham. Helen, having escaped from her drunkard of a husband with her five-year-old son, Arthur, arrives at Wildfell Hall. Gilbert, a farmer who lives nearby, describes the events from Helen's mysterious arrival until his marriage to her in the end.

Mother happened to hate this book. She always told me that it was a violation of social conventions, and that it should have never been published in the first place. She had ordered that all copies be removed from the manor; however, one of the female servants had ensured that one copy remained.

Despite my mother's hatred towards the book, I found it quite interesting. Not many women would have the audacity to slam the door on their husband's face. The most interesting part of the story was when Mr. Huntingdon died. He had abused his wife in the most horrible ways, and yet she was still able to feel pain at his death. I was not fond of the part where he pleaded for her to come with him to his judgement so that she may beg for his salvation.

Then, just as I put the book down, the last person I had expected to see entered the room. It was my old friend Matthew Caldwell. When I saw him, I was shocked and a bit confused. Certainly, he had not come here looking for me. After all, I had expected him to be furious with me for a long time.

"I thought that you might be here," he said, closing the door and walking up to me.

"You were actually looking for me?" I asked.

He nodded and handed me a letter, "I received your letter and I just want you to know that I understand."

I took the letter and carefully opened it. I was unsure of what he was talking about until I read the letter. It explained the whole situation from the time I first confronted Miss Hoffman to our time in London. At first, I was confused by this. There was no way that I had written this letter. That was when I realized who had.

"Sorry, I have been helping my father write business letters all week. I had forgotten which letters I had sent," I lied.

He nodded in understanding, "I am sorry that I did not let you explain in the forest."

"It is all right. I am accustomed to dealing with your temper by now," I assured him.

We stood there for a while in awkward silence before Matthew spoke again, "I hope that this has not affected our friendship."

"I would not dream of allowing it to do so."

He chuckled slightly and made his way to the door, "I should go. I promised my mother that I would look after my brother and sister."

"Keep James away from the wine," I warned him.

He looked back at me and smiled. "I will try." Then he was gone. I put my book back on its shelf and rushed out of the room. There was only one person who knew me well enough to write that letter. I only hoped that she was finished with my sister, so that I could thank her.

I found her just as she was leaving the music room with Caroline. As soon as Caroline had her back turned, I grabbed her wrist to stop her from leaving. She pulled me into the music room and closed the door behind us. "Did you speak with Matthew?"

I nodded. "Thanks to your letter, everything turned out all right."

"I am so glad that he is no longer angry with you."

"Tell me one thing," I requested. "Why did you write the letter?"

She looked me directly in the eyes. "I know what it is like to lose a friend, and I did not want you to lose him because of me."

I felt happier than I had in a long time. As strange as it might sound, Helene was the light of my life. I had to thank God for giving me that light. I knew that I would still be miserable had he not done so. "Have I ever told you how extraordinary you are?" I asked.

"I believe you may have mentioned it once before. Although I probably did not believe you."

"Well, I am going to ensure that you believe it for the rest of your life," I promised.

I had known that she was extraordinary from the moment I first met her, but I had never dreamed that she could be even more so than I had originally thought. Neither did I ever dream that I could love a person so much—especially one whom I had started out despising. This truly had been a tale of love and misunderstanding.

EPILOGUE

In the end, everything turned out all right for Helene and me. As expected, my mother was against the match. However, my father gladly gave me his approval and we were married five months later. Soon after, Mr. Johnson returned, and after Caroline explained what had happened between her and Mr. Johnson, Father allowed them to get married as well. He even purchased them an estate not too far from mine in Southampton.

In 1857, our first son was born. We decided to name him William, after Helene's deceased brother. Two years later, our second son, Edmund, was born. I always felt that I was the luckiest man in the world because I was blessed to have an extraordinary wife and two wonderful sons.

Matthew ended up marrying a charming young lady by the name of Abigail Stanton. He has often told me of their meeting, and as I recall, he said that they fell in love the moment their eyes met. Now I am not entirely certain, but I believe that he was exaggerating when he told me that.

Vincent dissolved his engagement to the woman our mother had set him up with, and eventually married a woman named Evangeline Weston. They were introduced through her older brother, who happened to be Dr. Weston, who had treated Vincent's arm after the hunting accident.

After Father's death in 1863, Vincent took over his role as Governor. His responsibilities did take up a large portion of his time, but somehow he managed to find time for his family as well. In my opinion, he was a much better Governor than Father had ever been.

Unfortunately, not everyone lived happily ever after. I am afraid to say that the marriage of Louise and James Caldwell was not a happy one. James turned out to be quite a bit like Mr. Huntingdon from *The Tenant of Wildfell Hall*. He became known as an outrageous gambler and drunkard, while Louise became known for her outrageous spending and shameful flirting.

The End

CPSIA information can be obtained at www.ICGtesting.com
Printed in the USA
LVOW08s0752270116

471609LV00001B/16/P

9 781460 280331